Balancing Act

Virginia M. Scott

Butte Publications, Inc.
Hillsboro, Oregon, U.S.A.

Balancing Act
© 1997 Virginia M. Scott

Editor: Ellen Todras
Cover and Page Design: Anita Jones

Butte Publications, Inc.
P.O Box 1328
Hillsboro, Oregon 97123-1328
U.S.A.

Scott, Virginia M.
      Balancing act / Virginia M. Scott
      p. cm.
      SUMMARY: A young woman (who is hard of hearing and
has trouble balancing) has a dream trip to Egypt jeopardized
by warring divorced parents, an uncertain boyfriend, and a
stepsister who despises her.
      ISBN: 1-884362-22-2

    1. Hearing impaired--Juvenile fiction.   I. Title.

PZ7.S368Bal 1997   [Fic]
                             QBI97-40276

DEDICATION: For my father

Acknowledgements

I would like to thank those who supported me
during a recent illness and encouraged me
to write this book:
Dr. Lowell I. Goodman, for his unflagging
concern and zest for solving medical mysteries;
Phyllis A. Whitney, novelist and friend, who
reminded me at a crucial juncture that one
must want to write badly enough;
and my husband Bill,
my anchor through the storm.

Don't walk in front of me;
I may not follow.
Don't walk behind me;
I may not lead.
Walk beside me
And just be my friend.

---Camus

Chapter One

Egypt! I had to pinch myself to believe I was really going somewhere so neat. Pyramids, tombs, camels—I'd see them all.

"It must be halfway around the world from Oregon," I said.

"I think it's a good 10,000 miles from here, Beth," my father told me. "We'll find out exactly."

"I can hardly wait!"

The trouble was, there was a string attached. My father and Susan, my stepmother of just a few months, broke the news when we were looking at travel brochures and talking about the trip over dinner at their house.

"You and Kari will share a hotel room," Dad announced so casually that it made the bombshell hit all the harder. Across the table from me, Kari gagged.

"She's going too?" my stepsister asked. She shoved away her plate of linguine as though it had suddenly turned into a nest of worms.

"Of course she is," voiced Susan so gently that I wondered why Kari couldn't be more like her.

Dad got up just then.

"Phone," he explained. Then he went into the hallway to answer it.

Kari shook her long blonde hair. I'd seen the gesture at school and knew nothing good was coming.

"Over my dead body!" she exclaimed as she sprang out of her chair.

"Don't use that tone of voice with me, Kari Quinn," Susan cautioned as her eyes skewered her daughter. *Good for you, Susan,* I thought.

"I'm sorry, Beth," she told me. I smiled weakly.

Kari was still standing beside her chair. When she turned to walk away, Susan asked, "Where do you think you're going?" Kari kept on moving toward the doorway, so Susan got up to follow. I never heard Kari answer her mother, if she did.

"Excuse me," Susan told me as she went after Kari.

They stepped into the laundry room just off the kitchen but left the door open. Anybody else might have heard them talking, but they might as well have been on the other side of the house, for all I heard.

It didn't take a Sherlock Holmes to guess that they were talking about me, though, and I'd never felt more like an outsider in their house. I mean, even in the best of times, the three of them had their routines and they knew where they fit in. No one had told me where I did—if I did.

The dinner table was a case in point. There were dirty dishes all over it. Was clearing them off Kari's job? Would she just use it as one more excuse to go after me if I tried to help out around here a little? She let me know over and over that it was *her* house, *her* mother, *her* life. I guessed they could just be her dirty dishes.

The leftover linguine on the plates looked revolting. A mint would taste good. Where was my purse? I looked around the kitchen and spotted it on a counter across the room. It was when I walked over to it that I realized I could hear Susan and Kari from where I was standing.

" . . . terrible . . . Beth." Susan's voice. Of course, when I heard my name, I was riveted to the spot. The only movement I made was to get into a better hearing position.

Even so, Kari said something too softly for me to hear.

Susan asked, "What did you say?" She sounded mad.

Kari spoke up. I missed a word here and there, but I got enough to piece it together. "Beth and I don't have anything to talk about. She's deaf."

"No, Kari," Susan corrected in a slow, matter-of-fact tone, "she's hard-of-hearing, and you know as well as I do that she hears you with her hearing aid on."

"You always stick up for her," Kari whined.

Susan shut the door then. Good, maybe she'd let that brat have it. I listened for more as I finally got out my mint, but I heard nothing.

I suddenly didn't care if they were Kari's dirty dishes. I couldn't just stand around with Susan and Kari in the next room talking about me. It gave me the creeps. Hey, I'm here, I wanted to shout. Sometimes I felt so invisible in this house. Angrily, I walked back over to the table and started clearing off the dishes, which I stacked on the counter beside the sink. Kari would just have to like it or lump it.

As I cleared the last glass from the table, I knocked the little stack of travel folders to the floor. When I picked them up, the top one stared back at me so invitingly that I couldn't help smiling. It had the Pyramids of Giza on it, and a camel was outlined against the largest of them in the final orange blaze of the setting sun.

I didn't want to go anywhere with Kari, let alone share a room with her, any more than she wanted to with me, but this was Egypt! I could almost feel the hot desert sand warming the soles of my shoes, almost taste the excitement of walking down the famous steps into King Tut's tomb, and almost see the golden columns of Karnak with their hieroglyphics all over them.

Yes, at any cost, I wanted to go. And whether or not Kari Quinn wanted me along, Granmary did, and it was Granmary who was sending us all on the trip.

Now, *she* made me feel like family. Susan's grandmother and I had hit it off from day one, so when she invited me to her house for high tea, as she called it, I started going pretty regularly. I guess it sounds weird, but I loved Granmary's stories, old-fashioned expressions, and the things she taught me. Everything happened so naturally at Granmary's, like the time I told her I liked her sweater and she told me she'd knit it herself.

"I could easily teach you how to knit, Beth," she told me with such enthusiasm that I thought I'd give it a try just to please her. I'd never counted on liking it, but once I got the hang of the basic knit and purl stitches, I found the repeated click of the needles relaxing. It was also sort of neat to watch something you were making grow like my first scarf was growing.

And since at eighty-nine Granmary couldn't see very well, I read to her. Sometimes it was the Bible, sometimes her favorite poetry, and often just the newspaper. She frequently fell asleep with a smile on her face while I was reading, which was my cue to tiptoe out.

My favorite thing was hearing her talk about the trips she had taken when she was younger. She'd been to so many wonderful places: France and Italy, the South Pacific, India, and Egypt, to name just some.

Just as I started remembering Granmary's tale of intrigue in an Aswan bazaar, Dad interrupted my thoughts by returning to the kitchen.

"You cleaned up. Susan will appreciate that," he said. He looked around the room. "Where are Susan and Kari anyway?"

I don't know why I covered for them, but I did.

"Oh, they stepped out for a minute. Maybe they were taking out the garbage." *Talking* it out was more like it.

....
4

"That was your mother on the phone," he told me. I could tell by the dead stop that he was debating about how much to tell me. Usually these days when Mom and Dad talked, there were "words" between them. There didn't even have to be a reason. Since they couldn't seem to be civil toward each other, I hated to think how Mom would react when I asked her if I could go to Egypt with Dad. I'd cross that bridge soon enough.

"Did she want anything special?" I ventured.

"Well, I guess we got our signals crossed. She wanted you home by seven." I looked at my watch: 7:20. There was a pause as Dad changed conversational gears. He added, "That reminds me. Did you ever ask her about the baby pictures? I don't want to take her to court to get some."

Oh boy, I hadn't. I knew Mom had a grudge a mile wide about the divorce, a grudge that was even worse now that Dad had a new wife, so I tried to keep some peace around our house. I knew asking for anything for Dad would set her off, and I was getting sick of hearing her talk about "that woman," as she called Susan, or "your father's new little family." There were no gray areas with Mom. Everything was black and white, and to Mom, Dad was the black hat guy in the divorce.

I wished Dad hadn't brought up the baby picture thing. I wished, even more, that he would just take care of things like that on his own, without asking me to get in the middle. It gave me that Oreo feeling, like I was that white stuff in the cookie being squished by both sides.

"It slipped my mind," I told him. Then I dove in with, "Dad, do you think it's even a good idea right now? I mean, I really want to go on this trip." Bringing up baby pictures before asking to go to Egypt would doom my chance for good. Would Dad understand, though?

"And you don't want to stir Mom up about anything else? Well, I guess I can understand that. Let it rest for now. It's time to bring up Egypt, you know. Don't put it off."

Whew! He'd understood.

"Thanks, Dad. I'll bring it up soon." We were planning to go during spring vacation, and since Mom was my custodial parent, I needed her permission. We also needed to take care of a lot of stuff, like passports and the right clothes for that climate, and Dad needed to buy airline tickets.

Susan and Kari walked back into the kitchen just then. Kari didn't look friendly, but at least she wasn't mouthing off.

"I have to get Beth home," Dad told them.

"I really enjoyed the linguine, Susan," I told my stepmother. Wanting to make peace, I added, turning to Kari, "Your garlic bread was great, too."

"Thanks," Kari said. Maybe she was also trying to smooth things over, because she added, "See you at school."

"Yeah. See you."

I was turning to go and must have missed something Susan said. It worked like that. I'd be hearing things just fine, as I had in their small kitchen, and then someone would say something into my bad ear and I'd miss it. Dad tapped my arm and pointed toward Susan.

"Did you say something?" I asked her.

"I just said we'll talk about clothes for the trip soon, Beth."

"That will be fun," I told her. "Thanks again for dinner."

We all said good-bye, and then I was on the way back to my house with Dad. My house . . . .

As we drove across town, I wondered how Dad

felt about dropping me off in front of the house that had been his until just about a year ago. It was a really pretty brick house with shiny black shutters and lots of rooms filled with Mom's favorite Queen Anne furniture. Dad didn't really get a whole lot in the divorce settlement, as far as I knew, unless you counted his freedom and his new family. Susan's house was all right but not nearly as big or in as nice a neighborhood as ours.

Dad must also have been thinking about the past, because he broke into my thoughts by asking, "Do you remember the time the carton of eggs fell out of your bike basket at this corner?" He pointed to a parking lot where a little mom-and-pop grocery store had been years ago. I was about eight when the incident happened.

Smiling, I replied, "Yeah, that was really a mess, wasn't it?"

"But even though those eggs never got to be Easter eggs, you did the only thing you could have by braking for that dog."

"He was so lazy," I said, remembering the old sheepdog. Slamming on my brakes had really thrown off my balance, that's for sure. There'd been egg all over the place. "I thought he wouldn't budge."

"And of course he did at the last minute," Dad put in. We laughed together at the memory.

What I really wanted to talk about I didn't, like asking if he was happy he'd left Mom and me, happy that he had a new wife and daughter. Who would have thought when I was eight and braked for the dog, or even a little over a year ago when I was fourteen, that Mom and Dad would split? "A marriage made in heaven," I'd heard some people describe it. "The perfect couple," others had said.

Each time I thought how they'd had it all and blown it, I just couldn't understand, just couldn't really forgive them for letting it slip away. I mean, they had each other, the house, me. Dad was a successful dentist, and Mom was a local television celebrity. They even looked great together, sort of like the bride and groom off a wedding cake. Mom was petite and blonde, while Dad was tall and dark.

Too bad I didn't look much like either of them. For the two-hundredth time, I wondered why I had to get stuck with such impossible black curls. A poodle with freckles and big boobs and hips that spoiled my outfits. "Hourglass like mine," Grandma Langford had consoled. The trouble was, hourglass had been in in her day. It bugged me that Kari had the kind of model's figure I'd always wanted.

"Almost home," Dad said, pulling me back. I saw the big stand of towering Douglas firs a few blocks from home and left all the comments and questions about the divorce unsaid. Thinking about Egypt was a whole lot better than wondering what had gone wrong.

"Do you think I can use my old passport for Egypt?" I asked.

"I've been thinking about that, too, and plan to do some phoning tomorrow. The one from four years ago when we went to England is still valid, I imagine, but you don't look eleven now. Since we need visas, we need to get cracking and planning."

"Which means it's time to tell Mom."

"Don't worry so much, Beth. A good mother wouldn't deny her daughter such a wonderful experience."

He couldn't see it in the darkness of the car, but I rolled my eyes. I'd heard him say that before and she'd turned whatever it was down flat, so that didn't do much to ease my creepies about the big confrontation.

"I hope you're right," I told him. Then, "We're here."

"Good luck," he told me as he leaned over to kiss me.

Then he was driving away.

Why hadn't I mentally written a script on the way home? I wondered as I turned my key in the lock. With leaden feet, I walked in.

"Mom, I'm home," I called out as I dropped my purse onto a chair in the foyer. Would I get the third-degree for just having been with my own dad and *them?*

I saw a light on in the kitchen, so I headed that way, expecting to find Mom in the nook having a cup of coffee. Instead, I found a plate of Toll House cookies and a note that read: "Had to take the cherry wool suit to Zelda."

In a way, it made sense, and in a way it didn't. Zelda was Mom's alterations lady, and as a person who went before the camera live five days a week on *Oregon This Morning,* Mom did have to look great. What I didn't get was why she'd had to make such an issue of my coming home right then. Power, I guessed. Power over Dad.

The idea of even a mental script suddenly didn't seem so hot. Since I didn't want to sit around rehearsing what to say about Egypt, and get more and more antsy, I decided to call Steph after munching two of the cookies.

There wasn't any describing Stephanie Ingraham. She was like the sister I never had, only better because we didn't fight all the time, as some sisters did. Steph and I just sort of thought alike and flowed with each other. I could be thinking something and she'd come up with the same thought, only out loud. Or I might be talking and not find the right word and Steph would come up with just the one on the tip of my tongue.

We'd played Barbies together, baked

gingerbread people at Christmastime with her grandma, put on fashion shows with our moms' heels and costume jewelry, and shared secrets by the zillion. I knew she was scared of spiders, and she knew I liked a little bit of light in the dark. Together we'd dreamed of doing something useful with our lives, like maybe being marine biologists or fighting AIDS, and together we'd laughed at each other and at ourselves.

She answered on the third ring.

"It's me," I said.

"Hey Beth," the familiar voice, sounding pleased, answered. Electronic things can be tricky with a hearing aid on, but with an amplifier on our phone, I could hear her pretty well. Anything I missed, Steph always filled me in on.

"Hey yourself," I told her.

"It's been a long time," she said, and I knew what she meant. We used to talk on the phone just about every night, but that had changed when Steph had moved with her family from our Portland suburb to the Seattle area at the beginning of the school year. At first, we'd talked long distance a lot, until our mothers freaked at the phone bills. Now we were down to about once a month.

"What's new in Bellevue?" I asked. She told me about her brother's engagement and making second-chair flute in band. Then she began a blow-by-blow description of one Ryan Keller.

"How's it going with Brad?" she asked after winding down a little about Ryan. When I didn't jump right in, Steph, being Steph, picked up on it and said, "Hmm. Do I detect trouble in paradise?"

"Paradise?" I laughed.

"Well, you could have fooled me."

Brad and I had been a pretty steady item, it's true. I didn't know how to explain what was happening between us, not even to Steph, because I didn't know myself. Things just weren't quite right anymore. The way we laughed at the same things was changing. The little thrill of having Brad's arm slip across my shoulder at the movies was turning to irritation.

"I dunno, Steph. He just seems so into himself sometimes. I've got to sort of work this out in my own mind before I can put it into words."

"I understand," she told me. One of the things I loved most about my old kindergarten friend was that she automatically knew when not to push me. Other times, she knew just when I needed a good, solid kick.

We talked a little bit more about other things. Then I said, "I've been saving the best for last." I paused for dramatic effect and went on with, "I'm going to Egypt!"

"Egypt! You rat. How could you let us chatter on and then casually tell me something so exciting?"

"Rat, huh? I'm glad you called me that with a laugh in your voice."

"Well? Tell me all about it."

That was the only invitation I needed, and as I told her how the trip came about and described some of the places I would see, I could tell by her questions and comments how happy she was for me.

"The thing is, it may not work out," I added. "I haven't told Mom yet."

Aware of lots of the divorce trouble, Steph commented, "Uh oh. How are you going to go about that?"

"Sort of play it by ear, I think. Oh Steph, Mom just has to let me."

That's when I saw, rather than heard, a movement at my bedroom door.

"I just have to let you what?" Mom asked.

Chapter Two

"Be with you in a sec," I called out to Brad, who had just pulled into the driveway. Even though I couldn't hear his car horn from most of the house, people told me he always tooted it. It was one of those times it was a drag not to hear right. I had to be so watchful. I was almost always ready in plenty of time, standing on the doorstep or looking out the window for him.

Today I was slower. After poking my head out to tell him I'd be right with him, I wolfed down a last bite of toast and grabbed my books and jacket.

"Hi," I told him as I finally slid into the car. Then I winced. Heavy metal blasted from his stereo, and my apology for holding him up never came out. Instead, a wave of irritation washed over me. I hoped he'd turn it down or, better yet, clear off. If he said his customary "Hi yourself, " I didn't hear him.

I wondered what he was thinking as I watched his fingers tap the steering wheel. To him, it was obviously great music, but for me the beat was downright painful, coming as it did through the hearing aid in my left ear. Instead of being music to me, it was a mind-blowing distorted blare that made me want to rip the hearing aid off. I winced again.

"Could you turn that down a little?" I asked as he pulled out of the driveway. Increasingly, he'd forgotten lately.

This is what I mean, Steph, I thought, *about Brad being so into himself.*

Maybe he hadn't heard me. The volume stayed up. Jarring as the sound was, I let it go for then, just to see if he'd remember. I could have turned my aid off, I knew, or reached for Brad's radio myself, but he knew what was what with the hearing aid and loud music.

Why can't you be more like Matt? I wondered.

I had met the Brownlee brothers about three years ago. Neither had paid much attention to their new neighbor at first, but Matt, who was interested in teaching the deaf, had noticed me because of my hearing aid. That had launched an unlikely friendship between a thirteen-year-old and a twenty-year-old that had lasted to this day. Matt was just always so tuned in to people's feelings and needs.

Brad had always been the kind of kid who pulled my braids and splashed that dirty stuff from mud puddles onto me. Then one day I started seeing flashes of Matt in him, and I decided that maybe this was what Matt had been like at one time. When Brad also started seeing me as more than that little neighbor girl, stopped bullying me, and asked me out, I accepted. We'd been going to movies and stuff for about three months.

In the car, the music continued. I wasn't trying to be a martyr or anything, but it was the principle of the thing. I wanted Brad to remember. Matt would.

Usually, the snowy form of Mt. Hood in the distance was a treat I looked forward to on the way to school, but I was too preoccupied to really see the scenery.

Not only was I irritated by the music—and Brad—but I was uneasy on another front, since I still hadn't said anything to Mom about Egypt.

Even though she had overheard me talking to Steph and had asked me what I'd meant by her "just having to let me," our conversation about the trip never happened. I could see right away that something was wrong for Mom, and when she asked if we could talk the next day instead, I'd said okay. When I had heard why she was rattled, I was glad I hadn't pushed. Zelda, Mom's alterations lady, had fallen right in front of Mom, and Mom was pretty strung out from having taken her to the hospital for X rays and, as it turned out, a special bandage on her badly sprained ankle. At least it hadn't been a break.

I might have had a chance before school, but Mom had a wacky schedule and left for the television studio very early, so the subject of Egypt was still hanging over my head. I would have to wait until dinnertime to bring up the touchy subject.

In the car, I couldn't stand that sound another moment.

"Brad!" I shouted, touching his shoulder so he'd know I was talking. He was going to make himself deaf if he didn't watch out.

"Huh?"

"The radio, " I mouthed, pointing to the offensive noisemaker.

"Sorry," he apologized as he turned it off, and his doe eyes, so like his older brother's, won me over. He was really cute, I thought, as he flashed me one of those heart-melting smiles. Just-turned-seventeen to my not-quite-sixteen, Brad was really better looking than Matt, who had a cowlick and a broken nose that had never healed quite right.

I was dying to tell him about Egypt, but since I hadn't told Mom yet, it didn't seem right. Instead, I asked him about his junior lit assignment. Since my good ear was toward him, I could hear him just fine without the radio on, so I listened to his reactions to *Cry, the Beloved Country* as we neared our school.

I liked it when we talked about stuff like that, but except for the book talk, it certainly hadn't been much of a conversation, I thought, as we drew up to Elston.

"We're here," I commented.

"Call you tonight," he told me as he kissed me lightly. Since we went to different parts of the building, we never walked in together.

With Egypt on my mind, it was hard to concentrate on history and English and stuff. I wanted, especially, to see Karnak and imagined towering columns and statues and vast halls under the burning sun. Just across the Nile from Karnak would be the Valley of the Kings and the tombs of the pharaohs. As best as I could, I pushed all the delicious images into the back of my mind for the day as I got down to the serious business of being a student, which for me also meant working to hear.

In some settings, like a quiet living room with only a couple of people, you'd hardly guess I have any hearing loss. In others, it really showed up, and school could go either way.

Even though I sat in front of the room to maximize my hearing, I missed certain sounds, especially soft ones like *s*'s. I sort of had to fill them in in my mind. Some teachers' voices came through very well. They just had a good pitch of voice for me to hear. Loudness certainly wasn't it. Mr. Petrillo for math last year, for example, had this really loud voice. I heard it fine, that's for sure, but words? It was more like a blitz of booms that had me reaching to turn down the volume on my hearing aid. Sometimes I couldn't win, though. If I turned it down too far, I couldn't hear him either.

Other teachers spoiled it by being pacers or talking into the chalkboard a lot. In those cases, the sound just sort of floated around the room or into the wall instead of getting channeled into my hearing aid. I'd learned to read lips as a way to beef up my hearing, but I wasn't as good at it as some people are because I usually just naturally relied on my hearing. Don't let anybody fool you. Lipreading isn't a snap. And of course, you can't lipread what you can't see, and teachers just weren't looking my way all the time.

My aid also had a maddening way of picking up coughs, rustling papers, and cracking knuckles, to name just a few distractions.

So, I really had to work, although with notetakers in some of my classes, I didn't really have to worry about missing anything too vital.

I knew there were special ed classes and interpreters, but I could hear too well for those, really. I wasn't deaf enough.

Right in the middle, that's me.

I hear, but I don't hear everything.

I also walk, but I don't walk right, thanks to the same illness that messed up my hearing when I was four years old.

Funny, I'm also stranded smack in the middle of two families. And I couldn't really get away from the family thing at school, because Kari was in a couple of my classes, and her locker was along the same wall as mine.

Anyway, that day English class went fine. We turned in our essays, and Mrs. Marshall spent most of the period cautioning us against purple prose.

With my stupid balance, I dreaded getting from one class to another, because if people bumped me hard, I could easily fall right over. Being sick had screwed up something called the vestibular area, and maybe some others, and I had to work hard when there was lots of motion around me or when I did stairs. I had some little tricks to help me along, like using my little finger, just barely touching it to the wall as I walked down the hallway, to steady me. No one even knew it. For me, the halls were also sort of lonely because hearing anything in them was tricky.

Since French was only three doors from English, I got there just fine.

"Bonjour, Simone," my French teacher greeted, using my French class name.

"Bonjour, Mademoiselle Latham."

I sat down and said hello to my friends Ashley and Karen.

"What's with them?" Ashley asked. Even though it was getting a little noisy in the room as everyone filed in before class, I could hear Ashley because she usually remembered to talk into my good ear. It helped that she wasn't more than two feet away.

"What's with who?" I asked, already suspecting whom she meant. When I turned to look at the door into the room, I said, "Oh."

Kari and two other girls were standing there, staring straight at me, snickering about something.

"What now?" I said, rolling my eyes. No doubt she was in a snit because Granmary had asked me to go along to Egypt, but I couldn't say anything to Ashley and Karen, even though I was bursting to, because I wasn't positive I really was going. It occurred to me at that moment how Kari would gloat if Mom didn't let me go.

Mademoiselle Latham made her usual expansive French gestures that signaled it was time to sit down, so even Kari and her group finally did. As class started, Ashley said, "See you at lunch."

It was a good class. We were studying the regions of France and their products. In her clear, precise French, Mademoiselle Latham distinguished between *La Champagne,* the region, as opposed to *le champagne,* the bubbly wine. I couldn't help remembering Granmary's description of driving from Paris to *La Champagne* and seeing a late-November hoarfrost heavily coating hill after hill of leftover champagne grapes with white. "Mumms, Taittinger, the finest grapes in the world," she'd said, "and I picked a little frozen cluster of them and savored their spoiled sourness."

We had a pop quiz on some grammar tied in with discussion, and then after saying we'd discuss Grasse and French perfumes the next day, it was time already for class to end.

Most of my classes that day were just as uneventful, and lunch was lunch, meaning it wasn't the same without Steph. Steph and I had been sort of like human magnets. We just sort of gravitated together wherever we went, including lunch. Ashley and Karen were our counterparts, so we all sat together at lunch. I still sat with them, but without Steph, I was sort of odd man out even though they were friendly and nice. I never heard much at lunchtime anyway. It was just too noisy.

As far as classes went, I never knew exactly what to expect at school, and this really held true for history that day. Mr. Lowe was one of my favorite teachers, and I loved history, but no one really knows what it's like not to be able to hear right, so they can't always anticipate what's going to bother a hard-of-hearing person.

To go along with our recent readings about Napoleon and the War of 1812, Mr. Lowe decided to play the *1812 Overture* that day. I don't quite remember what normal music sounds like, but the first part didn't sound all that bad, and even if some of the instruments had a weird, tinny sound, I could pick out many of them.

If only from the Fourth of July, probably everyone knows that finale with the cannon and bells and stuff. I might have gotten by if Mr. Lowe hadn't decided to turn up the volume just then. But he did turn it up. Way up, until it was even louder than the music in Brad's car had been.

Ouch! It felt like lightning scorching my ear. I hoped he hadn't deafened the only one I had left. Naturally, I turned off the hearing aid. There wasn't anything to prove here.

Well, as I said, Mr. Lowe is one of my favorite teachers, but even favorites screw up, and he really did that day.

I saw him remove the CD from the player. He walked back over near the front row of chairs,and I realized that he was looking at me expectantly. Did I do something wrong? No, it had to be my imagination. He wasn't looking at me at all, was he? Something made me turn around to see if maybe his eyes were locked on David Nyberg behind me, but when I turned, everyone was looking at me.

I wanted to melt right into the floor. What was going on?

Mr. Lowe walked over and tapped my chair. I suppose it was a gentle tap, but the vibration, conducted by the wood of the chair, whirred through me like a small explosion. And to think I was still reverberating from cannon and bells.

Cannon and bells! Oh no, my hearing aid was still off.

I quickly flicked it back on.

"What is your interpretation of the relationship of the music to the actual war, Beth?" he asked. That was just my kind of question, since I loved to interpret literature, art, and so forth. But music? Was he out of his mind? I hardly enjoyed the hurt of the sound before I turned the aid off, and I didn't hear it after I had. In fact, I was so busy fighting it that I certainly hadn't tried to interpret it. Should I make up an answer?

"Umm," I stammered.

Mr. Lowe was waiting. So were twenty-six others. I could almost feel the heat of so many eyes boring into my back. I felt sort of sick. Couldn't we have a fire drill now? As the seconds ticked by, I knew I had to say something.

"To tell you the truth," I told him in an under-statement, "my hearing aid didn't pick up the music very well." I didn't want to make him feel funny. He was usually so sensitive.

Frowning, Mr. Lowe scratched his head and said, "I thought I had it turned up." With that, I felt my face turn tomato-red as I heard the awful sound of laughter behind me.

Then it was Mr. Lowe whose face was red. "Oh no. It was too loud."

I nodded. "I turned the hearing aid off," I whispered.

He looked so apologetic that I feared a big, dramatic speech right there in class, but just to me, he said, "See me for a minute after class." Then he moved on to Cheryl Meier for the answer I couldn't give.

Studying the xylem and phloem of a carrot in biology seemed like a piece of cake after history, and even algebra didn't seem so bad.

I stopped at Granmary's on the way home from school. Since Brad got out an hour earlier than I did so that he could get to his after-school job at an auto supply place, he was a one-way driver as far as school was concerned. Fortunately, even with my balance problem, I liked to walk as long as it wasn't too slopey or crowded. And even though it was January and the dead of winter, our Portland area climate wasn't always all that cold; even the east wind off Mt. Hood didn't feel too sharp in the winter sunshine.

Granmary's home was a small, one-story wood house, painted white.

"Just knock and come in the back door," she'd told me, so that's what I did. I walked through her tiny kitchen and found her engrossed in an elaborate crochet pattern.

"Hi, Granmary. Is that going to be a lace collar?

It's beautiful."

She looked up from her plum-colored wing chair and smiled in a way that seemed to smooth away almost ninety years of care. Even though she was very wrinkled and small, she had a queenly bearing. Her hair was always done up just so in a French twist, and her clothes, although not fancy, were carefully pressed.

"Thank you, dear. No, it's not a collar this time. I'm working on a set of placemats for a nephew and his bride. How are you coming with your scarf?" she asked, mentioning my first knitting project. I told her it was getting long and that it was fun to do.

"Good. In no time, you'll be ready to learn some fancy stitches." She lay her work on the lamp table beside the chair. Even with my hearing aid, I heard a heavy sigh. She seemed tired for this time of day. "Why don't you fix us some Earl Grey?" she asked. I'd also come to fancy her favorite blend of tea. I put the water to boil and went back into the living room.

She had her head resting against the back of the chair. Well, I wouldn't stay long today, since she seemed tired, but I wanted to thank her for including me in the Egypt plans. She heard me walk back in. Maybe she wasn't that tired, at that, as she sat up in her usual erect way, looking eager to talk. How she loved her company!

I leaned over and kissed her forehead.

"My, what's that for?" she asked.

"Oh, Granmary, you know. Egypt! Thank you so many times over for thinking of me. You know how I love everything about Egypt. Going would be a dream come true."

"You remind me so much of myself," she mused.

I rattled on some about the places in Egypt I wanted to see most. They were all places on the tenta-tive itinerary, all places I'd heard Granmary describe from her own trip there so many years before.

I didn't hear the kettle whistle from the kitchen, but Granmary did. I poured our tea and brought it back in, along with the plate of finger sandwiches she had fixed earlier. They were always such cute little shapes, with the crust cut off, and the filling ranged from cream cheese and olives to chicken salad. Today it was sprouts and the thinnest ham on whole wheat bread.

As we nibbled and talked about Egypt some more, I told her again that going would be a dream come true.

"*Would* be? Why not *will* be, Beth?"

"Well," I told her, putting down my cup of tea, "there's a major hurdle. I haven't said anything about the trip to Mom yet." Granmary didn't know all the details of Mom and Dad's state of open warfare, but she did have some idea, from the things I'd said.

"That's a hurdle, all right," she told me, "but I think if you approach her sincerely, Beth, and tell her how much you really want to go, she will come around. But ask her instead of telling her. And do it soon."

"I'm going to tonight."

"Good. More tea?" She pointed to the china pot beside our sandwich plate.

"Thanks," I told her. "I'll pour."

As I did, I noticed her reach into her pocket. When she withdrew her right hand, she had something cupped inside it.

"Here," she told me, handing me something hard and cold. "It's yours, Beth, no matter what your mother decides."

I looked into my hand and saw the most unique ring I'd ever seen. It was an Egyptian scarab of the most wonderful shade of blue, in a heavy gold setting. It looked expensive, like it ought to be an heirloom.

"Oh, Granmary, I can't. It's the most beautiful

ring I've ever seen, but shouldn't Kari have it?" Kari was, after all, her real great-granddaughter.

"Nonsense!" she exclaimed. "Kari has the gold signet ring—her favorite—and she will get more after I'm gone. I shall never forget your eagerness to listen to my tales, never forget the enthusiasm you had when I told you about the giant stone scarab at Karnak. No, dear, this is meant to be yours.

"Besides," she said with a little laugh, "Kari never liked the beetle carved into the lapis."

That did it then.

I hugged and thanked her, and then I slipped the ring onto my finger.

"Perfect," she pronounced.

Now if I could just come up with the perfect way to tell Mom.

Chapter Three

It was probably lucky that I'd eaten several of Granmary's finger sandwiches, because my stomach was too tied into knots to eat much for dinner that night.

Mom and I talked about generalities at first. She told me about interviewing Ariel Downs, who had written several steamy romances and was hot with romance-novel readers. I told her about the *1812 Overture* fiasco.

"That must have been terrible," Mom agreed. "I think you handled it well."

All along, when it came to my hearing loss and balance problem, I couldn't have asked for a more supportive mother. She always remembered to talk into my good ear, for one thing, and she never made me feel ungraceful. Sometimes when I got down about those things, it was Mom who made me see the humor in a situation and Mom who pointed out my strengths.

She was a lot better about it, really, than Dad. Even though he kind of accepted my hearing loss, it bugged me that he often didn't even remember which ear was totally deaf. The balance thing was worse for him to accept, maybe because he was athletic and valued grace and physical stamina. I don't know. He just seemed to want me to be what I couldn't be, and that hurt.

One time he even talked Mom—against her judgment, from the fights I'd heard about the subject—into sending me to charm school to help my balance. I did learn how to pour the perfect cup of tea, and I could fold napkins in twenty different and interesting ways. I learned proper introductions and how to write perfect little thank-you notes. But that wasn't why Dad had sent me. No, he wanted me to "walk right" and, who knows, maybe even turn into a female jock.

Talk about fiascoes! As I said, I have some little tricks to help me walk and keep from falling. It's not that I lurch like Frankenstein's monster, but I don't walk with the fluid grace of a model, either, and because something in my head is haywire, it would take a new head, not deportment lessons, to correct the problem.

Just remembering Miss Hamilton made me want to throw up.

"That's the ungainliest curtsey I've ever seen, Beth," she said in front of the whole class. She even had to repeat it twice. To me, she seemed to be breaking all the rules of etiquette by calling negative attention to me in front of everyone. "You just have to hold that back straight, bend, and get down there. Would you insult Her Majesty?"

The way she said it made me feel like a total dunce, and I felt tears burning behind my eyes. Would it get worse? The curtsey was bad enough. Was I going to cry in front of everyone, too? I had practiced and practiced that dumb thing at home, and I just couldn't get low enough without needing to touch something to keep from falling on my face. Heaven forbid that I should ever come face-to-face with real royalty, or I'd get sent to the brig for lack of deference.

Of course I fell right in front of Miss Hamilton and eleven other twelve-year-olds. When I described the situation to Mom and Dad and told them I didn't want to go back, Dad called me a quitter and said I hadn't applied myself, but Mom understood and insisted that enough was enough.

Fortunately, I still hadn't met the Queen.

But would Mom be as understanding about this Egypt thing?

At the dinner table, she commented, "You aren't eating very much tonight. Are you okay? Listen, honey, I'm sure Mr. Lowe will go back to being his usual sensitive self."

"I'm fine, Mom. I think you're right about Mr. Lowe. The chicken's great, but I'm just not very hungry," I told her. "I stopped at Granmary's, and her little sandwiches were more filling than usual."

Since Granmary was Susan's grandmother and part of Dad's new family, it always amazed me that Mom accepted Granmary. It really all started because Granmary had been a steady viewer of Mom's morning television show. They had met after Granmary had written Mom a very gracious letter about a segment on senior citizens. When Mom expanded the topic and interviewed Granmary for the new segment, the two women had just hit it off.

"That's okay," Mom told me. "The chicken will be good cold later on."

"Mom," I said. "I hope you'll let me keep it, but look what Granmary gave me today." I held out my hand so that she could see the scarab ring.

Mom reached for my hand, turned it back and forth, and said, "It's a wonderful piece of jewelry. The blue even matches your eyes. I know how you adore anything Egyptian. Wasn't that sweet of her to give it to you?"

That's my cue, I thought.

"I really love the ring," I told Mom. "And you're right about my adoring anything Egyptian." *Here goes.* "Mom, you'll never guess what."

"What?" she asked as she sipped coffee. *Now don't freak out,* I silently pleaded. She looked so calm sitting there in her pink sweats. A little of the TV personality remained, even with the sweats, in her diamond tennis bracelet, for instance, and her studio-done hair, but she looked so kind—so motherly—right then. Maybe it wouldn't be so bad.

I felt my palms. They were sweating.

"Beth?" she prompted.

"Well, I can't believe it, Mom, but Granmary's giving me the chance to actually go to Egypt. You know it's my dream trip."

She set down her coffee cup.

"A chance to go to . . . . Why, whatever do you mean? Is Mary strong enough for a trip like that?"

"Uh, no. I wish she were," I said.

Mom looked kind of blank for a few moments. Then the face that had looked so gentle moments ago twisted into a look I'd seen all too often since Dad had walked out.

"You don't mean what I think you do, do you?" she asked. She had a hands-on-her-hips tone even though we were sitting down. The look on her face might just as well have asked me if I'd gone bonkers.

"With Dad," I nodded, "during spring vacation."

There was a big pause. Was she trying to picture it? I could tell she didn't like what she was seeing in her mind's eye. What was so terrible about my taking a trip with my own father, for Pete's sake?

"Just the two of you?" she asked.

"Well . . . no." I hated to bring their names into it, but I had to say it. "Susan and Kari would go too."

"And they want you along?" she asked skeptically. She went back into herself for a moment. I wondered if this time she was trying to picture the quartet of us together in Egypt. As she came out of her mini-trance, something within her shifted gears. The blue eyes that charmed so many people from the other side of a television screen met mine defiantly.

"You're not going," she pronounced so quietly that it had the force of a shout.

....
27

Can't you ever be decent about Dad? I thought. It had been about a year since he had left, but had that mellowed Mom? No way! I took a deep breath and told myself to keep outwardly calm, not to get baited and react in a way that would axe my chances for good.

"Won't you at least think about it, Mom? It's the chance of a lifetime for me. And Granmary is so happy and excited about my seeing the things she did when she was younger."

Please, please, I prayed.

But I think I saw the bad news in her face before I heard the awful words.

Much more firmly, she repeated, "Beth, you can't go."

Hope went out of me then as surely as the air leaves a popped balloon. I saw Karnak, the Valley of the Kings, and the Pyramids of Giza evaporate into thin air. To think that I'd come so close to seeing them made me absolutely sick.

Something snapped inside me. I knew Mom was just saying "no" because of the way she'd written off Dad. I couldn't stand looking at her right then.

Staring at one of her Delft plates over the table in the nook, I said, "It's not fair."

Since I didn't want some diatribe about her idea of fairness, I got up and started walking toward the stairs, on my way to my room.

Pyramids . . . *poof.*

Mummies in museums . . . *poof.*

People speaking a different language and dressed for the desert . . . *poof.*

The more images I saw vanishing, the angrier I got. And all because my mother and father, who had managed to live together peacefully for fifteen years, for crying out loud, now hated each other.

I wanted to get up to the haven of my room, but I

hadn't quite reached the stairway when I saw motion behind me from the corner of one eye. Why did Mom have to follow me now?

"Beth?" she said. I stopped in my tracks as hope surged. She was changing her mind. I just knew she was. Maybe Dad was right. She wouldn't, couldn't, deny me such a wonderful opportunity.

"You can go upstairs in a snit," she said, crushing any fleeting hope, "but just remember to put the blame where it belongs."

Something exploded inside of me. Instead of running up the stairs, I looked her square in the eye, and what I had meant to save for just the right time just spilled out.

"Mom, is it true that Dad doesn't have any of my baby and little girl pictures?"

I regretted it the moment I'd said it.

"What makes you ask that?" she tossed at me. She took a few steps into the living room. I followed.

"It came up."

"Came up?" she challenged. Wasn't that like her? With her eyes boring into me, Mom went on with, "Who were you talking to about me, Beth? Your father?"

There it was again. I hated the way she spat out the word *father* as though it were poison biting into her tongue. Her blue eyes deepened to navy, and I knew there was more to come.

"Not that woman, I hope."

"What difference does it make if your name comes up?" Was I some kind of informant? It wasn't exactly as if Mom had state secrets to hide.

Shaking a finger at me, she warned, "Don't you ever say a thing about my life to those people. Your father gave up any right to know when he walked out. My life is my life now."

"Mom, I just don't want him to take you to court over this."

"He threatened to do that? Of all the ridiculous things!" she screamed. I jumped back. Her explosion of words blared through my hearing aid. As I shook my head to free it from the unpleasant ringing, Mom grabbed a satin pillow from a chair and threw it across the room, just missing her treasured Lladró figurine of the little girl and her kittens.

Wow, she was really upset. I mean, throwing a pillow in this room where everything was just so was a big deal for Mom. The flower pattern on the wing chair matched the pattern of the window swags, and the same flowers popped up again in some of the scatter pillows on the davenport and loveseat, which were the exact shade of green as the green in the patterned material. As I saw the big mirror over the fireplace, I breathed a sigh of relief. At least the pillow hadn't gone that far and hit either antique ginger jar on the mantel. Mom and the thrown pillow were the only things out of harmony with the room, unless you also counted our feelings.

What seemed like half an hour passed as she stared at the wall. As much as I wanted to get up to my room and be alone, I still wasn't sure what was what with the pictures, and I had to know.

"If you're too busy," I told her, "I'll sort through them. All he wants is copies, you know, not the originals." It wasn't like he was trying to rob her of anything. But I'd hit a nerve. She reminded me of one of those battery people who suddenly come to life.

"Don't touch those pictures, young lady!" she ordered in her best no-nonsense voice as she spun around to face me. She wore such a mask of anger that I saw the truth. Dad didn't have any pictures. Mom had hoarded them as though I'd been an immaculate conception and only she was entitled to remnants of my past.

Were we having a stare-down? Whatever was happening in her mind, she finally looked away and then went over to the loveseat and sat down just as something lurched in my stomach and I thought I was going to throw up. I almost wished I would so it would land on Mom. Why was she being so stupid about these pictures?

"Okay, I won't," I promised, "but don't you think Dad has as much right to them as you do?"

That did it. She shot off the loveseat and stood, glaring, as she shook her finger at me again.

"You are talking about rights? I'll tell you something. He doesn't deserve them, Beth. He didn't have any trouble gathering his clothes, his precious books, and some other things when he left me for that woman. If your baby pictures meant anything to him, why didn't he take some? So you see, they are mine by all rights. I value them."

Why hadn't Dad taken them? She had me there, and I felt the wind die out of my sails.

"Let's get something straight," she continued. "What goes on in this household is our business and our business alone. I don't want you ever sharing anything—and I mean not . . . a . . . thing—that goes on here with your father and his new family. He gave up the right to know anything when he left. He threw us away, Beth, and he's no more entitled to information about this home than he is to any possession he left behind. Your loyalty is to me. I'd never leave you."

Then she turned on her heel and stalked off to her bedroom.

Chapter Four

Brad's radio was off when he picked me up for school the next morning. After yesterday's trouble with Mom, he looked so normal sitting there in his jeans and jacket, which was about the same wonderful chocolate brown as his hair. His eyes were a darker, almost black-brown and had impossibly long lashes that any woman would die for.

"Hi," I told him as I slid in beside him. He looked at me appreciatively, and I realized I had on an old wool sweater I'd accidentally shrunk when I hadn't read the "dry clean only" label. Thanks to Mom, I didn't feel so hot. I'd sort of thrown together the day's outfit.

"Hi yourself," he answered. As I heard his voice, I thought how strange it was. I mean, after yesterday's noise in the car, it was a relief to be able to hear him. The trouble was, I just didn't feel much like talking.

"I'm sorry I didn't call last night," he apologized.

Hadn't he? In the wake of the blow-up, I hadn't even missed Brad's call.

"That's okay," I assured him.

After Mom had stalked off, I went to my room, where even the normally cheery yellow walls hadn't eased my hurt and anger. In fact, the dam broke once I'd closed my door, and all of a sudden I was bawling for the lost trip and crying even harder for my lost family.

How could I ever forget coming home from visiting my grandparents in Santa Rosa, California? Both my parents had seen me off at the airport, but by the time I'd returned ten days later, bursting with exciting things to tell them and with no greater care in the world than finding out from Steph what had happened while I was gone, my happy family had broken apart. Only Mom picked me up.

It was like a charade on the ride home. Dad had a tennis match, she lied. Then when we got home, the whole floor seemed to cave in as she told me that he had moved out.

I had spent a few months feeling so mad at Dad that I wouldn't even see him at first. He had visiting rights, though, and gradually I got into a new routine with him. Inside, I was still so hurt and confused and furious at him for walking out on us that the few times he'd tried to explain, I just told him I didn't want to hear about it. "Another woman," Mom had explained, and when Dad finally introduced me to Susan, it sort of fell into place.

In the car, Brad's hand touched my knee.

"Earth to Beth," he said as I jumped.

"Huh?" I asked.

"You were a million miles away," Brad observed.

"Oh, I guess I was. I was just thinking about the divorce," I explained.

He rolled his eyes, but I was sort of touched when he asked, "Do you want to talk about it?"

I did want to, in a way, but not with Brad, I realized.

"Not really," I told him. Then, not waiting to cut him off after he'd shown interest, I added, "There's nothing new with them. They just can't stand each other, and I feel caught in the middle."

"Yeah, that must be tough. Maybe they'll mellow out in time."

Without really thinking, I sighed and said, "I wish I had time, Brad."

He gave me a sideways glance and raised his eyebrows.

"Do you have a fatal illness or something?" he joked. When I didn't laugh along with him, he looked

....

33

at me briefly again and got more serious. "What's going on?" he asked.

I had to talk to somebody about Egypt. Steph was almost two hundred miles away, and I couldn't keep calling her. I looked at Brad. He seemed so sympathetic just then that I told him about the trip and Mom's refusal to let me go.

"I just feel so crushed," I told him, as the full force of Mom's answers came flooding back.

But he totally missed the point of my feelings.

"Egypt?" he commented. "That seems like a funny place to go."

A "funny" place? What was the matter with him?

"How so?" I asked. My surprise at his reaction, at least, had the effect of holding back the tears that had been bubbling somewhere deep inside me.

"Oh, I dunno," he said. "Ruins. Tombs. The past." For all the enthusiasm he put into the words, he might just as well have said: Liver. Spinach. Curdled milk.

I looked at him. He wasn't putting me on. He really didn't see anything exciting about going to Egypt. Well, what difference did it make if Brad Brownlee found Egypt tantalizing or not. I did.

Ruins. Tombs. The past. All the lost images flitted through my brain then, and I felt the tears again, only this time in my eyes.

"But what a glorious past," I said in a wavering voice, thinking of Granmary's word for the land and long history.

I guess he heard something catch in my voice. He pulled the car over and stopped.

"Come here," he told me, inviting me into his arms. I knew he didn't really understand my sense of loss, but his warm hand patting my head was comforting just then. I was starting to feel a little better when he spoiled it by trying to kiss me. *Not now,* I wanted to say. Instead, I just turned my head so that his kiss landed on my cheek instead of my lips. He got the message.

"Hey," he said as he looked at his watch, "we'd better be on our way or we'll be late."

I was dry-eyed by the time we got to Elston.

"It'll all work out," he told me as he let me out. Then, "Hey, are we still on for Friday?"

"Sure," I told him. "Thanks for listening."

When I saw Kari in French, I was never so jealous of anyone in my life as I was of her at that moment. I mean, *she* was going to Egypt—with my father at that—and I was staying home. I rubbed the scarab ring like a worry stone. Boy, would she gloat when she found out I wasn't going. Well, I wouldn't let her in on that just yet. It wouldn't hurt her to worry a little about sharing a hotel room with me.

I tried to concentrate on Mademoiselle Latham's discussion on essences from Grasse, but nothing she said really grabbed my interest. There was just too much else on my mind.

Kari Quinn. Until her mother had married my father, she'd been just another girl at my school. I had neither liked her nor disliked her. We just never moved in quite the same circles. While I was caught up in activities with Steph, mostly, and Karen and Ashley, Kari was into sports and hung out mainly with the other girls in basketball and track. She had the long legs and height to do both. A natural athlete, I guessed she was.

And she'd been okay to me, if not actually palsy-walsy.

Once Dad had married Susan, though, Kari really had it in for me, for some reason. It wasn't just the way she snubbed me when she saw me, either. No, that wasn't enough for Kari Quinn. She had to bad-mouth me, too.

Maybe one of the worst things about being hard-of-hearing, instead of really deaf, is that sometimes you hear when other people think you don't. I don't make a habit of listening in to people's conversations, but sometimes when you hear your own name, you just sort of can't help it.

"I saw Beth at the movies," I overheard Kari blabbing to her friends one day. Her voice carried right into my good ear. "She was falling all over the aisle, and what does a deaf person get out of a show anyway?" There was some truth to that since my balance was really bad on a slope in the dim light of a theater. I did get some of the dialogue, though, and since I wasn't a dunce, I could fill in most of what I missed.

Then came the part that really got me.

"It's pretty clear," she went on, "why the guys take her out. What else does a handicap like her have to offer except boobs that stick out to *there?*" She held her hands out about a foot in front of her own flattish chest.

A *handicap?* The word twisted into my heart like a dagger. Why hadn't Kari just said "freak"? That's how she saw me. And to think she was my new stepsister!

When I saw Gretchen and Lia laughing along with her, it was even worse. Why didn't they stick up for me?

I was getting choked up all over again right there in French class. Fortunately, my teacher's voice pulled me back: "Tomorrow," she said in English, "we will begin a menu-making project. *En francais.* Be thinking about a name for your very own French restaurant. You may call it anything you want to. *La Belle Epoque,*" she gave as an example. "Or you may even name it after yourself. *Chez Simone,*" she gave as another example, winking at me since that was my name in class. I smiled back.

Then French was over. I usually left right away to give myself plenty of time to get to the next class, but since the last thing I wanted to do was to come face-to-face with Kari, I took my time gathering my books and stuff together. The seconds ticked by. Even Ashley and Karen, famous for their poking around, had left. It must be safe, I decided. Besides, I couldn't afford to wait any longer, or I'd be late.

My heart sank as I got up to leave and saw her still there. It was almost as if she knew I was feeling rotten and wanted to get under my skin. Was she a witch? Like a matched set of gargoyles, Gretchen and Lia were standing with her near the door. Too bad it was the only way out.

I took what I hoped was only a silent gulp and started toward the door.

Just walk on past them, I coached myself.

"Chez Booze," Kari said sarcastically as I neared them. I didn't have the slightest idea what she was talking about. *Booze?* Wasn't that what my uncle called whiskey? Should I say something about it? But Kari flipped her long hair, fiddled with her notebook, and sauntered out with her friends. Had she been talking to me? Who knew?

My other classes were Kari-less until I got to biology, which also happened to be one of the ones I had a notetaker for. I knew Mrs. Middleton couldn't do much about her soft voice, and fortunately Janelle Jacobs, my notetaker, was really super. She was a master, for one thing, at sketching diagrams, and she seemed to sense that I wanted a full-spectrum notetaking job. Not only did she make sure I had assignments and the heart of class discussions, but she included the little jokes and things that made me feel included. They were the things other kids heard and probably took for granted. Sometimes they were weird. I remember one time, for

37

example, when Kenny Mickelson had suddenly run out of class. Another kind of notetaker might have left me wondering, but Janelle had written in that she'd heard him barf from the back of the room. True, I didn't need to know that to help me with biology, but knowing sort of put me on a plane with the rest of them. I just liked to feel included and to know what was going on.

Today, though, Janelle's chair was vacant when I got to biology, and when she still hadn't shown up by the time class was ready to begin, Mrs. Middleton came up with a brainstorm.

"Kari," I heard her call. I didn't get the rest, but when I saw her motion to Kari, I wanted to disappear. Was she actually singling out Kari to sub for Janelle? What else could go wrong? I looked back to where Kari always sat and knew my suspicion was right. She was getting her stuff together. Mrs. Middleton came up close and said something just for me. I heard her only in bits and pieces—something about Kari being one of her best students, I think. I smiled weakly. I guessed it made perfect sense to Mrs. Middleton, but I knew Kari was pretty unenthusiastic about it when, scowling, she plopped into Janelle's chair.

I didn't normally hate being hearing-impaired. I mean, I'd lived with it for as long as I could remember, and it just was a part of me. But right then I hated it with everything I had. Being dependent upon *her* just did something to me. It's for less than an hour, I told myself. I could stand it for that long, couldn't I? But it was worse than I'd imagined.

I knew Kari hated me, but I couldn't believe it as I watched her start writing what Mrs. Middleton was supposedly saying. It wasn't about the structure of carrots and the other veggies we were studying.

Did you know your dad and I play tennis together all the time? she scribbled. *We're really getting good.*

38

I like going to Moeller's for ice cream almost as well as our playing.

These aren't notes, I wrote in my own notebook. Then I shoved my message under her nose.

I saw her smile. She picked up her pen and began writing more about the things she was doing "all the time" with my dad.

I finally just stopped reading her dumb "notes" and tried my best to lipread Mrs. Middleton. With all the scientific words, though, it was pretty futile, especially since she was a floor-pacer as she spoke. I just sat there fuming. Kari was trying hard not to laugh. It was all I could do not to reach over and tip her chair over. How could she be so cruel?

And was it true that she and my dad were playing tennis "all the time" now? The image of the two of them hitting balls back and forth cut into me. Me? I'd fall flat on my face if I tried to run toward a tennis net or reach to hit a ball. It was bad enough that Kari was doing something with Dad that I'd always wanted to do, but couldn't. But Moeller's? That was our place. How could he?

I thought biology would never get over. When it did, Kari rushed right out. Fortunately, I got some notes from Sammi Grady, which was lucky, because Mrs. Middleton had announced a test. I'd never know if Kari would have let me come totally unprepared on test day.

I could hardly wait for school to end that day, just to get away from Kari. Of course, I had Mom to contend with at home, which was another story, but even though I didn't like the way Mom acted about Dad, I sort of knew where she was coming from. With Kari, I wasn't sure.

Computer lab, without Kari being in it, would be a breeze, I thought. The trouble was, I had to walk down some stairs to get there, and with my balance the way it is, stairs can be tricky. Our school was split-level and didn't have elevators, but of course it was adapted for wheelchair users with ramps by the stairways. Ramps are the worst things of all for me, though, since their inclines really mess up my equilibrium, so I use the stairs as the lesser of two evils. No one ever thinks about the balance-impaired when they design buildings.

I have to think when I walk, and every time I go up or down the stairs, I have to concentrate in a step-by-step approach, almost like doing a detailed class assignment:

1. Balance the books in the crook of one arm with the purse on the opposite shoulder just so.
2. Hang onto the railing for dear life.
3. Don't stop midway up or down the flight.
4. Try not to get bumped.
5. Don't talk to anyone.
6. And concentrate, concentrate, concentrate—one step at a time.

Usually it works.

Today, about halfway down the steps, I felt some people pressing in from behind all of a sudden. I guess they didn't like my slow, deliberate descent and were impatient to get moving, which brought me to step number four: Try not to get bumped.

I tensed and gripped the railing harder. *Ease up!* I wanted to shout as I felt them so close behind. *Stop pushing me. I'm working with everything I've got to stay upright.*

Stopping to let them by would violate step number three: Don't stop midway up or down the flight.

Someone's book jabbed my back, and I could taste real fear in my mouth. Did I look scared? Did they feel my fear and find it hilarious? Whatever, I heard laughter. Was it at me?

Now wait a minute! Wait just . . . a . . . minute here!

More laughter.

I wanted to turn around and face them and say, "You dolts. Don't you know how lucky you are to be able to walk down the stairs, gossiping, carefree, with balance centers that don't demand step-by-step approaches to something so seemingly simple? Why are you in such a hurry? You, you dolts!" I wanted to scream at them.

But I couldn't even do that, because I knew from unfortunate experience that turning my body on a busy stairway was bad news.

Watch it!

I'd let my mind wander only momentarily, and I swayed. I clenched the railing in a death grip.

Someone pointed at me and said something I didn't get as I lurched. Then in one of those times I wish my hearing aid hadn't worked, it picked up something terrible.

"There goes Boozy Beth." The voice came into my good ear and cut into me like a knife.

Snicker, snicker. This time from behind.

"Boozy Beth," the voice echoed in my thoughts.

Take a step. Hang on, I coached myself.

"Boozy Beth," the voice echoed again in my thoughts as tears blurred my vision.

Take another step, hang on, concen—

I was flying down the last three or four steps . . . falling . . . falling . . . .

Let me crack my head open and die on the spot, I silently begged the powers that be, but they didn't listen. Instead, I sprawled in an ignominious heap at the foot of the stairs. My books, papers, and purse, which had come open, scattered around me. Was that a *tampon* rolling out of my purse? I really was going to die on the spot.

Boozy Beth. Boozy Beth. The awful name gonged and gonged in my mind.

As I looked up, I saw three girls giggling as if I were an attraction in a sideshow. They didn't even try to help.

"Clumsy me," I said as nonchalantly as I could, trying to salvage the moment. The trio laughed again and walked on. Time to fix their ugly little faces in the restroom, no doubt. And there I still lay, a real, live Raggedy Ann. At least I wasn't really hurt.

At that moment, Tom Edelman, a dreamy senior, stopped to help me. If I hadn't been so mortified, it might even have been romantic when as I brushed myself off, he retrieved my books and flashed me a smile.

Julie Schmitz was there, too, and scooped the tampon up and into my purse with a wink before, I think, Tom saw it.

People did care.

But I'll never forget the faces of the laughing trio. One of them belonged to my stepsister, Kari.

Chapter Five

I almost stopped at Granmary's house on the way home from school, but I decided I wasn't in the mood to break the news that Mom had axed the older woman's gift of the trip. At least Kari's "notes" and my fall at school had shoved thoughts of Egypt into the recesses of my mind for awhile.

I slid the scarab ring round and around my finger as I walked. Granmary's gift was so like her. I hadn't known her long, but she just always seemed to think of other people and automatically knew what they'd like.

Granmary Sealy was something else. You picture octogenarians sitting in their rockers, crocheting. Well, Granmary did sit in a rocker sometimes, and crocheting was almost a passion with her. It's just that there was so much more to the woman. It was Granmary who had gone to the city council with proposals to make our suburb more accessible to wheelchair and cane users, Granmary who had spearheaded the fight to save a stand of ancient oaks, and Granmary who had read stories to preschoolers at the public library until her eyesight had gotten too poor a few years ago. I knew from her stories, too, what a sense of adventure she had. How many people, after all, take their first hot-air balloon ride for their eightieth birthday?

Of course, with her arthritis, poor vision, and heart trouble getting to her, she was slowing down, but that spirit of adventure, even if it was sometimes just trying a new crochet pattern, was still alive and well. It's one of the things I loved best about Granmary. It would have been so nice to have seen Egypt for her sake, so that she might have tasted my adventure through my stories, reliving her own in the process.

Mad at Mom again for spoiling it, I opened the back door. Sometimes she was home after school and sometimes she wasn't. Today I hoped she wouldn't be. I really didn't want to get into it again, and I didn't trust myself not to get down on my knees and beg.

No such luck. She was fixing tea at the kitchen island as I walked in. Instead of her usual coffee mug, three delicate French teacups and the pretty matching teapot with the pink flowers on it stood on the counter-top. She must have some people in from her show, I thought. Well, good. I could escape to my room without a hassle.

"Hi," I told her. A major cold shoulder would just make things worse.

"Hi, Beth," she greeted. To my surprise, she was all smiles. "I have someone in the living room and thought you'd like to join us for tea."

"Tea? Thanks for thinking of me, Mom, but I have lots of homework."

"Come on," she coaxed as she busied herself putting the cups and pot onto a tray. "I can guarantee you it's someone you'll want to say hello to."

I doubted it, but I couldn't get up the stairway toward my room without being seen, so I didn't have much choice. Although Mom didn't have what I thought of as one of her studio suits on, she was wearing a pretty, matching slacks and sweater set, in a blue that comple-mented her eyes and shoulder-length frosted hair. Not too dressy, I thought, and yet not the sweats she usually put on the minute she got home. The mystery guest must be somewhere between her producer and an old neighbor, I guessed.

As I walked into the living room, I thought Mom must be putting me on. There was no one there. I set my books onto a lamp table, and then as I walked further into the room, I saw her sitting there where the green wings of the big chair had hidden her small form.

"Granmary!"

"Hi, Beth," she said. Mom, who was pouring our tea, just smiled. As I gave Granmary her cup, she winked at me.

What was going on here?

I didn't realize that I was still standing until Mom said, "Sit down, Beth. Mary and I have something we'd like to tell you."

I did as she asked. Could it be? Had I bagged the trip after all? No, it couldn't be that, I thought, as I remembered Mom's reaction the evening before. No way would she let me go with my father and "his new little family." But they did have something to tell me, and they really had my attention. Granmary had never been here before.

"You are probably wondering why I'm here, aren't you, dear?" Granmary asked.

"I'm just glad you are, Granmary. Having tea at my house for a change is nice."

"That it is," she agreed, "but I didn't come just to have tea."

"You certainly didn't," Mom laughed. "Beth, Mary talked some sense into me. You can go."

"Go? You mean, on the trip?" Was it really happening? I looked from Mom to Granmary and back to Mom again. As I saw the wonderful truth in their eyes, I sprang up and ran over to hug Mom.

"Oh, thanks, Mom. I'll never forget this." What magic had Granmary worked? I ran over and kissed her on the forehead. "And thank you again . . . for every-thing."

"You just have the time of your life, and that will be thanks enough," she told me. And then we were telling Mom about all the wonderful places I would soon be visiting.

"She's letting me go!" I excitedly told Steph on the phone that night. Mom had made an exception to the long-distance calling rule.

"I knew she would." Steph sounded almost as keyed up as I was. "You worry about too many things, kiddo." We talked a little about my trip—I still had to pinch myself to really believe I was going, after such a close call—and then Steph herself had a surprise for me.

"I was just going to call you," she told me. "How would you like some company next weekend?"

"You mean you? Steph, are you coming down?" A three-hour drive away could seem like an ocean apart when it separated best friends.

"Yeah, if you want me. Mom and Dad are going down to visit some old friends."

"Want you? I can hardly wait! There's so much to tell you."

"That was my line," she said with a little laugh. "Mom and Dad are staying in Beaverton, so I'll be close by again."

"No way! You're staying at my house." I knew Mom wouldn't mind, and I had a strong hunch her folks wouldn't either. We agreed to talk it over with them.

"Let's not make them mad by talking too long," we also agreed before hanging up.

On a cloud from Mom's change of heart, even with Kari as a thorn in my side at school, I breezed along the rest of the week, except for a little cloud over clothes. Mom assumed she would be taking me shopping for some things for Egypt, but so did Susan, according to Dad. He was really relieved when he'd phoned and I'd told him I could go. I would face the Mom vs. Susan issue later.

Brad and I usually went to a movie on Friday nights. This Friday, though, the Trailblazers were playing basketball on television, and since I was into Blazermania as much as Brad, it wasn't any sacrifice to give up our routine. In fact, I welcomed it for more reasons than one.

Not only did I look forward to seeing if the Blazers could maintain their hot streak, but things hadn't been too good between Brad and me lately. Last Friday, in fact, we'd had a fight about the French film I'd suggested we see. The characterizations were so sweet and poignantly true to life that I had loved it. Brad didn't like subtitles, for one thing. He also had written it off as "sappy" and "snaily," meaning he thought it moved too slowly. He was entitled to his opinion, and I certainly didn't expect him to like everything I did, but he got too far into it, until he was running down my taste more than the movie itself.

He didn't even like Egypt.

At least when it came to our favorite basketball team, we were totally in sync.

Since Mom wouldn't be home, we couldn't watch the game at my house. She had a rule that I couldn't have guys in for stuff like that without her there, and this was hardly the time to take a chance on making her mad.

"My parents will be home," Brad said. "Would it be too much of a drag to share our evening with them? We could order in a pizza."

"Sounds perfect." I liked his parents. Since they lived only four houses down the street from us, I knew the Brownlees as neighbors as well as Brad and Matt's parents.

The four of us had a great time in their family room watching the Blazers trounce Houston on the big screen. Houston was having a terrible time shaking off our defense even though the Rockets were giving it all they had.

"They're really hot," I said.

"Playoff material," Brad agreed. His parents weren't quite the fans we were and seemed amused by our enthusiasm. In fact, by the start of the third quarter, with Houston trailing badly, they decided to call it a game.

Mrs. Brownlee, aware that I can't hear voices very well with the television as background, grabbed the remote and muted the volume for a moment.

"You two will be all right if we go out for a bit, won't you?" Mr. Brownlee asked. "Maggie thought the store might be quiet right now."

Brad's mother chimed in with, "We won't have to grocery shop tomorrow then."

Brad and I, caught up in the game even if it wasn't that close, urged them to go. Waving as they left the room, Brad's father turned the volume back up and handed the remote control to Brad.

Our pizza arrived shortly after that.

"I'm stuffed," I pronounced as I finished my third slice. Brad had turned me on to pineapple and Canadian bacon pizza. I knew his folks didn't go for it. Maybe they'd already eaten.

"I'm not," he said as he reached for another slice. Just about that time, Portland missed a lay-up. It seemed to change the momentum of the game, and what had been a shoo-in suddenly turned into a real contest.

When it finally got down to the last minute, it was anybody's game. Brad was on and off the sofa like a jack-in-the-box, while I sat there white-knuckled as the clock wound down.

"I can't stand this," I said. I couldn't hear Brad's voice just then over the excitement on the screen, but amazingly Portland was behind two points with just under two seconds left in the game. At least they had the ball. Would they try to tie it and go into overtime or go for a three-pointer?

During a time-out, Brad muted the sound and we briefly debated the issue of the two- or three-pointer. Again, I thought how in sync we were about things like this.

Then the time-out was over and they were back. Eyes glued to the screen, we both stood up, hearts racing. *Here goes,* I thought as Portland passed the ball to its best three-point shooter. We all but knew what he was going to try, but could he pull it off?

The ball was suspended in mid-air for what seemed like minutes, and then it was arcing down. It was going, going. It went in!

"All right!" Brad yelled as he turned to me and hugged me hard.

"I knew they'd do it," I said happily.

And then Brad was kissing me. When it went from celebrating our team's victory to something else, I pulled away. He reached for the remote and flicked the TV off.

"I could stay like that forever," I heard him say.

"Let's watch the post-game show," I suggested, not wanting to get into anything heavy. I sat back down and he sat beside me.

"Let's not," he countered. "Here, have another slice of pizza. I'm going to." And with that, he did. I drank a little more cola and started talking about the three-point shot that had sewn up the game.

"Blazers 108-Rockets 107," I said with pride in Portland.

"I love the way you get so stoked up," he told me. "Did you know your eyes sparkle when you talk about the Blazers?"

"You get pretty wound up, too, you know."

"Die-hard fans. That's us," he said as we both

laughed. The good mood led to another hug. Then he was kissing me again.

"Oh, Beth," he said softly, and something in his voice made all my mother's warnings rush back. I pulled away, but before I could get up, he took my arm and spoke again.

"Isn't it time we made a real commitment to each other, Beth?"

"Commitment? What do you mean, 'commitment'?"

"Let's talk about it." There was something odd in his voice.

"I'd better go," I said. I got up.

"No," he said as he reached out a hand to stop me, "don't go. There isn't any reason why we can't talk about this."

He had a point, I supposed, and his parents, after all, would soon be back from the market.

"All right. Let's talk about it," I told him as I sat back down, leaving quite a bit of room between us.

He looked at me squarely and said, "Is it wrong for friendships to change and for people who care to want to go on to the next stage of a relationship?" he asked.

"No, it's not wrong to feel this way or that way. I just think what people do about their feelings can be wrong, though. To me, a commitment means real caring and respect."

"Let me show you how much I care then," he said.

"I wish you would," I replied, not realizing he'd meant one thing and I, another.

The words were no sooner out of my mouth than he was all over me.

"Brad!"

He didn't seem to hear me. He touched me some

place I didn't want to be touched. I said his name again, and when he still didn't respond, I slapped his face so hard that my hand stung. As he looked at me in disbelief, I got up and raced out of the room.

With my balance, I didn't run very well, and the tears that were blinding me didn't help. I felt a thud and a woolly sweater before I heard the voice.

"What's going on?" it asked.

"Matt!" I exclaimed in total surprise. Wasn't Brad's brother supposed to be in his apartment near the college?

He gently pushed me away from his sweater so that our eyes met, and the reassuring way he looked at me made me start blubbering. As if Matt, too, were remembering our long friendship, he pulled me against him for just a second and then held me out at arm's length.

"Wait for me on the porch," he told me. "I want a word with my brother."

Sort of numbly, I sat on the porch swing in the chilly night air, trying to figure out how a Blazers game had gone from being so much fun to total disaster.

Matt looked very angry when he returned.

"Come on," he told me, "I'll walk you home." He knew me well enough to understand that even with my hearing aid on, the darkness screwed up my balance even on flat surfaces. The streetlights were set far enough apart that it was pretty dark between our houses.

Matt took my elbow to guide me as we walked in total silence past one of the houses separating the Brownlee house from mine. The last thing I wanted to do was to start crying again, but my eyes smarted afresh when I remembered how nice Brad had been in the beginning and how into himself he was now. Had the kind, considerate Brad only been an act or my imagination? Had he ever even liked me?

Then I remembered Kari's words to her gargoyle

....
51

friends when she'd called me a *handicap*. "What does a handicap like her have to offer except . . . ."

A little cry traveled from my heart. Matt must have heard it. He stopped walking and spoke.

"Do you want to tell me about it?" he offered.

He was the guy who had comforted me when I'd come home from the orthodontist's with shiny new braces on my teeth. Surely I was the ugliest girl in the world. Matt had found me sobbing on a bench in a far corner of our yard, and he had somehow made the world right again.

I didn't think he could do it now.

"Here," he said as he wiped a tear off my cheek with the back of his hand.

"Thanks," I told him sort of shakily. Then, "There's not too much to say."

"He made a pass at you, didn't he." It was a statement rather than a question. He looked at me searchingly and must have seen confirmation in my expression.

"I just can't talk about it right now, but would you do something for me?"

"Sure," he told me with a smile.

"Would you tell Brad not to pick me up for school on Monday?"

"That bad, huh? Well, of course I will, Beth." He paused a moment before adding, "And remember, if you ever need an ear, I'm here."

It did help . . . a little . . . and I smiled.

Then he walked me the rest of the way home.

Chapter Six

The phone rang twice on Saturday. It was Brad, Mom informed me each time, but I didn't want to talk to him. With a mother's radar, Mom knew something was wrong, but although she asked if I wanted to talk, she didn't try to pry anything out of me, either. It would all work out for the best, she consoled.

I tried to lose myself in homework. Then I made a stab at cheering myself up by looking through a big coffee-table book on Egypt. Try as I did not to think about Brad, he crept into my thoughts like a thief and robbed my day of any real happiness.

On Sunday, I went with Mom to a dollhouse and miniature show. Mom's penchant for Queen Anne furniture didn't stop with her own house. She liked to collect little, scaled-down Queen Anne-style chairs, which she had on a shelf in the powder room. I'd liked them too, ever since I was tiny, and going to collectors' shows together could be lots of fun.

When Monday rolled around, I didn't expect Brad to pick me up, so I got up early, expecting to walk to school. The doorbell rang as I was finishing my cereal.

Let him stew, I decided. Since I still had plenty of time to get to school on my own, I poked around rinsing out my bowl.

The doorbell rang again.

Did I want any kind of future with Brad Brownlee? The funny thing was, I wasn't sure. I mean, I didn't like this fairly new downside of our relationship, but we'd also had some good times. Didn't he deserve, if not a second chance, at least the opportunity to apologize?

"Coming!" I yelled. Would he look like normal, or would he look sorry that things had gotten out of hand? I didn't get to find out.

"Jeeves at your service," Matt said, bowing formally.

"Jeeves?" I raised my eyebrows. He was acting weird.

"Your chauffeur, ma'am."

"What are you doing here?" I asked.

"Driving you to school," he told me. "May I?"

"Of course, but what I meant was, why aren't you at the college?"

"In a nutshell," he explained, "my apartment has some structural flaws, and I had to move out temporarily while they're being repaired. I'm back at Mom and Dad's for now.

"But that's not all," he continued. "I'm actually going back to high school as of this morning."

"Back to high school? Matt, what are you talking about?"

"Come on," he told me. "Grab your hat and get your coat, and I'll tell you in the car."

He was starting his student teaching, he explained. A grad student now, Matt was following up on his ambition to become a teacher of the deaf.

"There are classes for deaf students at Elston High," he told me. Although I'd known he was in a program, I guess I had never stopped to think about student teaching or where he might be doing it.

"So, you're going to be at my school. That's great."

"To tell you the truth," he confessed, "I feel like a little boy going to kindergarten for the first time."

"I can imagine. But Matt, I can't think of anyone

....

more suited to this profession than you. Even as a high
school kid yourself, you knew it was what you wanted
to do. And for good reason," I added. "You're a natural."

"More, more. I'm more confident already."

I might have given him just a few of the scads of
examples of how sensitive he was toward the hearing-
impaired—I knew firsthand, after all—but we were
pulling up at the school.

As we did, I noticed Brad's little green car whip
around the corner. Matt saw it too, and I guess he also
noticed the frown that screwed up my face. The way
things had gone still stung.

"Remember," Matt told me, "if you need to
talk . . . ."

"I know. Thanks. And if you need to talk . . . ."

"Thanks," he echoed.

Of course the girls at school talked about the two
new male student teachers that week, and it was fun to
hear some of them say how neat Matt was and know that
he was my longtime friend.

As for Matt and me, we fell into a new routine.
Just as he had that first morning, he continued to pick
me up for school every day. We never ran out of things
to talk about, whether it was something light and fun,
current events, or something deeper. I could tell *he*
didn't think Egypt was a weird place to go, either.

Why couldn't Brad be more like his brother? I
wondered again.

The differences became more and more apparent
with Matt picking me up in Brad's place. It was little
things like Matt always remembering to have the radio
off so that I could hear him, or knowing not to drop me
off on a slope. Matt had ideas about everything under
the sun: world peace, racism, the economy, to name just
some. But although Brad and I had sometimes talked

about major issues, they were always his pet issues, not mine. He always steered it that way. Matt, on the other hand, wanted my opinions, wanted to talk as much about my favorite topics as his own.

Had I been fooling myself, thinking that Matt had been like Brad at seventeen? Apparently so.

Brad was being so stupid. If I thought it hurt to see him at school and have him ignore me, it really drove a spike through my heart when he finally noticed me and called me Boozy Beth right to my face. How could he?

When Matt picked me up for school the morning after that, he didn't start the car right away.

"Beth," he said, "it's probably none of my business, but I overheard what my brother called you at school yesterday. I'm extremely disappointed in him and embarrassed to think that my brother would act that way. He feels rejected, you know."

"*He* feels rejected! He's thrown me in the trash can, Matt, thrown me away because he couldn't have his way."

"It must feel that way. It's his loss." Matt reached for his big black notebook and pulled out a sheet of paper. It was typed with what looked like a poem.

"What's that?" I asked.

"A poem written by a hearing-impaired student when she was about your age. It's a copy, so you can keep it. Read it over when you have some quiet time to think about it."

"All right," I told him as I took it from him and slipped it into my notebook.

I'm not sure how we got into the topic of dreams.

"You are making yours come true," I told him, thinking of his longtime ambition.

"I know, and it feels great. Have you thought any

further about what you want to do? I remember that you always wanted to be a nurse."

"I did want to for a long time, but I realize it's not practical with my hearing loss."

"Don't be so sure," he told me.

"Well, I am, Matt. I may not know exactly what I do want to do. I mean, I know I want to go to college and all. It's just that I thought about nursing for a long, long time, and I even did some research. I can't take the chance of not hearing at exactly the wrong time. I mean, even if I got in and made it through a nursing program, I think I'd owe it to my patients to hear better in all kinds of situations than I do. A patient wouldn't always talk into my good ear. And with masks on—stuff like that—it just seems too risky. I'm not giving up. I just believe in knowing my strengths but also knowing my limitations."

"I think that's very wise. In fact, did you ever stop to think that recognizing and accepting one's limitations is paradoxically a strength?"

"Yeah, I guess that's right. But I do have some wild dreams. You wouldn't believe . . . ."

When I trailed off, he coaxed me into telling him.

"Just one wild dream," he said.

"Hmm." I thought for a moment. Then I decided which one to tell him. "It sounds crazy in light of my balance and all, but I've always had this fantasy of putting on a really floaty chiffon dress and dancing a Viennese waltz with someone in a tux. I watch the pros whenever they're on television. Of course, I know I'd fall all over the place. I took ballet and it was hopeless. But that doesn't stop the ballroom dancing dream."

"I've always admired Fred Astaire and Ginger Rogers," he commented.

"Oh, me too," I said, amazed that he hadn't laughed at me.

I switched the conversation back to his teaching. Now that he was getting into his student teaching, he was more relaxed, and I enjoyed hearing about it from him. The more I heard, the more I realized I knew next to nothing about the deaf, which is funny since I'm basically hearing-impaired myself. Even with my hit-or-miss hearing, I took talking for granted, for one thing, and I couldn't really imagine signing all the time the way Matt's students did.

"I can't imagine not using words," I told him. "You know, like *scintillating* and *oubliette.*"

"*Scintillating* I know, but *oubliette*? Where did you get that one, Beth," he asked with amusement in his voice, "and what does it mean?"

"I wasn't trying to show off."

"I know."

"Okay. An oubliette is a certain kind of dungeon," I explained, "and I read it in a short story—maybe F. Scott Fitzgerald. The word just sort of grabbed me and has stuck with me."

"I can see why," Matt nodded.

"Well, anyway, how would you sign those words? I mean, there's a prison, a cell, a dungeon. How would you differentiate an oubliette in signs?"

"You'd fingerspell it. There's a visual alphabet made with the fingers, called fingerspelling," he explained. He pulled the car over to the curb then and stopped. "Here, let me show you. This is *A*," he told me as he made a fist and held his thumb up straight, "and this is *B*," he went on as he changed the position of his fingers. "Anyway, it's a lot like writing something on the blackboard or spelling it out loud. Only this is a visual thing. You'd make your *oubliette* like this," he finished. Then his fingers seemed to be flying.

"Then why doesn't everybody just fingerspell everything?" I asked.

"Well, for one thing, it would be so cumbersome that holding a conversation would be extremely taxing. I mean, think of the way we talk, Beth, and consider how slow it would be if I greeted you with: "H-E-L-L-O, B-E-T-H.""

"Yeah," I laughed, seeing his point, "it'd take forever if we spelled everything out like that."

"That's why people who use sign systems such as American Sign Language use a combination of concept symbols and a few fingerspelled words. The concept symbols, which are also visual, of course, make it go a lot faster than plain fingerspelling would be. Instead of spelling out dog, for example, the concept symbol, or sign, goes like this." He slapped his thigh a couple of times, like some people do when they're calling their dog.

"That's neat. You mentioned sign systems, plural. I thought signs were signs."

"People in general do seem to think of American Sign Language, or ASL, as *the* language of the deaf, and it is very widely used, but there are other systems. Some of those follow English word order."

"You mean ASL isn't English?"

"It's really a language unto itself, Beth. It has its own grammar and syntax, but so, too, do foreign languages. I know you're taking French. I never took the language myself and can't use it as an example, but I did take Spanish. I know you've been to Mexican restaurants. All right, think of their menus: *taco grande*. The adjective is after the noun. We'd put it first. Well, ASL and English have differences just as Spanish and English do. ASL doesn't follow English word order."

"Why don't all signers use these other systems then? The ones like English? I mean, we live in a mainly English-speaking country."

"Let me get the car rolling again," he said as he pulled back on the road. Then he went on with, "You're thinking in terms of your own hearing loss. You're hard-of-hearing," he explained, "but essentially you function as a hearing person. You developed an English language base before you had any hearing loss, Beth, and you hear new words all the time. You're comfortable with English. I'm still just a student, but from what I know, a lot of factors play a role in the language development of a child. Just one of these, the age the child lost her hearing, is so crucial, because the deafened child who has a verbal language base tends to be more comfortable with words than the child who never had one. Other factors that play a role in language development include the child's IQ; family background; schooling, if any, before the onset of deafness; residual hearing; and the child's general health.

"Lots of little children," he continued, "are born with little or no hearing at all, or they lose it before they formed that base. It makes a lot of difference. Hearing children learn language by imitating sounds that little deaf children miss, so visual communication systems are often more natural for them."

"I feel sorry for them," I told him.

"Well, don't. Maybe some of them don't have their *oubliettes*, but sign systems like ASL are most efficient languages. Just watch two people having an animated ASL conversation, and you can notice the way they emphasize through their body language and facial expressions. You'll see that they aren't just getting by. It is a dynamic, evolving language just like English. So, Beth, they have their special ways of communicating just as you do with your favorite words. It's just different. Hearing-impaired people, whether they are totally deaf or mildly hard-of-hearing, are individuals with individual needs, abilities, and potentialities. You need to fit the communication system to the person."

"So what's right for one person isn't necessarily right for another," I put in.

"Exactly."

We were pulling up at Elston already.

"Boy, we got here fast," I said.

"We'll continue this conversation some other time," Matt told me. Then he briefly changed back to our earlier conversation about Brad.

"Keep your chin up, Little Bird," he told me as I was getting ready to get out of the car. He put a finger under my chin and gave it a light chuck. "Don't let Brad or your stepsister get you down."

"I won't," I said.

Little Bird. It was Matt's nickname for me from years ago. I'd found a baby robin on the ground, almost naked of feathers. He looked so scrawny and delicate and in need of love. I picked him up and had him in my hand wondering what to do. I didn't see a nest around, and I knew the Ponzeks' cat would probably get him if I left him on the ground. And then my new neighbor Matt had shown up. He'd take the bird inside, he told me, warm him, feed him, and then let him go when he was ready.

Maybe I looked a little bit like that bird myself at that point, but for whatever reason, Matt had sometimes called me Little Bird from that day on.

And the robin had survived.

Now he was telling me to keep my chin up and not let Brad or Kari get to me.

Of course, that was easier said than done. Although I didn't hear Brad calling me names that day, I did have a run-in with Kari.

I was deep in concentration at my locker, since a major history test was coming up that day and my personal problems were getting in the way of facts and dates that were just sort of floating through my mind aimlessly. I could only hope they'd coalesce at the right time.

"Beth! Beth . . . five times," a voice yelled impatiently.

Kari. I turned to face her. It was noisy in the hallway, and I could use all the help I could get, including reading her lips. What could she want?

"Why didn't you answer me?" I think she said. Her accusing stare suggested I'd committed some kind of terrible crime.

It wasn't my fault I didn't hear right.

"Why do you think?" I asked. I'd moved around so that the sound of her voice was going into my good ear.

"Come on. I was only a foot away. You heard me."

If there was one thing I hated, it was being accused of pretending I didn't hear. Was she going to call me Boozy Beth, too?

"Think what you like," I told her. We stood staring at each other as seconds ticked by. Then I added, "My right ear is dead. It's noisy in here. You were talking into my right ear at first. Need I say more? Let's talk later. We'll be late for class."

She said something as she reached into her purse.
That's right, Kari, I thought, *talk to the purse, not to me.*

When she looked back up, I could hear her better again.

"Here," she told me as she handed me a check from my father. "Your dad said it's to reimburse you for the passport picture fee."

I thanked her and reached for the rectangle of paper. As I took the check, Kari's eyes zeroed in on my right hand and grew wide. I saw that they were fastened on the ring on my middle finger.

Kari pointed to my hand.

"Where did you get that?" she asked, glaring daggers. She had to have known the answer.

"Granmary gave it to me. We'll talk more later, okay? I don't want to be late." This wasn't the time or place to talk about it. Besides, I needed the extra time to walk to class.

She turned slightly, away from my good ear, and I didn't get what she said, but I think she told me I'd better bet we'd talk about it later.

She huffed away. Later on, I might as well have been invisible to Kari in biology. At least Janelle was back as notetaker and I didn't have to endure Kari as her sub.

Thank goodness Steph was coming. She would be a breath of fresh air.

Chapter Seven

"I can hardly stand it when I see him walking down the hall at school," Steph told me as we sat on some big cushions on the floor of my room. Her eyes gleamed like peridots with that wonderful zest that somehow defined my best friend, and I felt a rush of emotion. Steph must have seen it. "Why are you looking at me like that?" she asked.

"It's just so good to have you back home. It's been a long time," I told her. She agreed.

She looked pretty much the same. Her red hair was still long, and she had it tied back into a ponytail with a green scrunchy that almost matched her eyes. She'd commented that her chest was still "pancake city," but it went with the rest of her slim body.

She said I looked the same, too, only that my hair was a little longer, and I thought how weird it was that I could look the same and yet have been through so much since Steph had lived nearby. I'd gained a stepmother and stepsister, befriended an eighty-nine-year-old woman, learned I was going to Egypt, found a new boyfriend and broken up with him, and dealt with name-calling from both my new stepsister and my ex-boyfriend.

After Steph had filled me in on her new school and I'd told her about my trip and Kari's awfulness, we got down to the topic of guys. That's when she'd told me all about Ryan and the way her heart flip-flopped when she spotted him in the halls.

"He sounds really neat," I said for not the first time that evening. To use a Granmary word, Steph was really *smitten* by that guy. "Just don't get yourself in too deep."

"Yes, Mother," she said.

"Well, dear," I said in what I thought was a motherly voice, "you have to watch these teenaged boys and their—"

"Hormones," we both said in unison as we giggled.

"Speaking of hormones," she said, "you're awfully quiet about Brad. You mentioned on the phone that something wasn't quite right. Want to talk about it now?"

"Yeah," I told her. How did I explain Brad? I paused, trying to think what to say. I guessed I'd start at the beginning. "You know, he was always the bully next door. I never even liked him."

"He's really cute, though."

"He is, and maybe that's partly how I ended up going out with him when he asked me a few months ago. We had fun at first, Steph, and then, I dunno, he just started getting so into himself."

"For instance?" she asked.

"Well, movies, for one thing. At first, we went and we talked about them, and he seemed interested in the ones I liked. We traded off. One week, he'd pick, and the next, I'd choose. His were usually action movies, and you know how I like foreign films. I don't think two people have to always like exactly the same things to get along. It should be give and take. But I actually liked some of his choices."

"Uh huh. What went wrong?"

"Well, he just gradually started picking apart 'my' movies. I didn't mind that as much as the way he implied that my taste was bad. I didn't tell him he had a one-track mind for car chases and explosions and stuff like that. He could have swallowed a few of his complaints just for my sake, don't you think?"

"Yeah. What else?" she prodded.

"Just the way he talked, Steph. More and more,

it got to be about himself: his opinions, his favorite issues, his homework assignments. It was like, 'Hey, I'm alive, too,' I wanted to say."

"Doesn't sound so good, Beth."

"I know, and that's only part of it. When he tried to push me into something I didn't want, he wouldn't stop, Steph, and I slapped him right across his cheek. I mean, I really let him have it."

"I say good for you," she told me. She seemed to be trying to picture it. I saw her expression change as she went on with, "You don't mean he tried to . . . *you know?*" I'd known Steph for so long that I knew exactly what she meant.

"Well, I didn't wait around long enough to be positive, but I'm pretty sure he was trying to . . . *you know.* The bottom line is that he didn't listen to me, Steph, didn't respect me enough to listen, and that's what ended it for me."

"But you got out of there okay, didn't you?" she asked with real concern in her voice.

"Yeah, I did. Anyway, it's over between us. The funny thing is, I miss him. He could be fun sometimes, too."

"I don't know why, Beth. You're a lot better off without him. Maybe you miss the good times you had in the beginning."

"That's probably it," I said. "It's just too bad Brad isn't more like . . . ."

"Yeah? Do I detect someone else waiting in the wings of your heart?"

"Oh no. I was just thinking about Brad's older brother, Matt. I think you met him once."

"I think maybe I did. Was he the one who was teasing us about our Halloween scavenger hunt?"

"He's the one. He's so much more sensitive and mature than Brad."

"He's a lot older than us, though, isn't he?"

"Yes, so don't get any ideas about him and me. He's just my good friend, Steph. He's been driving me to school, in fact, since he's doing his student teaching at Elston."

"You don't have him for a class, do you? That would be weird to ride with him and then have him teaching you."

"Oh no. He's a special ed teacher. In fact, his field is the education of the deaf. You know how the school has some classes."

"Yeah," she said. Then she started waving her arms.

"What was that?" I asked.

"Well, it's a small world, I guess, but my new school offers sign language, and I've been taking it. I signed, 'You're my friend, and I'm glad to be here.'"

"Well, I'm glad you're here, too." The sign language thing, so close on the heels of my discussion with Matt, intrigued me. "How do you like signing?"

"It's really neat," Steph said enthusiastically. "In fact, I'm not sure I might not want to do something with it—maybe teach like your friend, interpret or something."

"That would be great. I know a teensy bit of ASL," I told her as I slapped my hand twice to my thigh.

"Dog?" she asked. When I nodded, she laughed and added, "Boy, that's a useful thing to know. Were you talking about your stepsister?"

"No," I told her, sharing in her laughter. "Matt sometimes talks about his teaching in the car on the way to school," I explained, "and he just happened to show me that sign as an example."

"I've always thought of you as sort of anti-signing," Steph said.

"Not really. It's just my background. I don't think it'd be something I'd want to use with friends or even at school in classes, but I don't know . . . ."

"Well, you love French, and you could approach it as a foreign language, just like you have French."

"Yeah, that's the context, all right."

"Do you want me to teach you a little?"

"Sure," I told her.

We worked on it some right then and there. An hour later, I knew how to fingerspell part of the manual alphabet, and how to greet people and make a couple of comments. I also knew one dirty phrase.

"Your teacher taught you that?" I asked.

"Nope. Just picked it up from a student in a more advanced sign language class."

"Boy, they've got signs for everything," I said. It really was an all-purpose language.

"All joking aside," Steph said, "they really do."

Our easy talk continued for hours. We also had a bite or two with Mom, who had always liked Steph, and then it was off to a movie for the two of us.

Being with Steph was so good. I got nervous, for one thing, walking down the slanting aisles of a theater. With my balance, I had to use my step-by-step theater aisle approach, much as I used my step-by-step stairs approach in other settings, and I was terrified of falling, falling, falling like some roly-poly Humpty Dumpty all the way down the length of the the-ater. Steph, though, had known me since kindergarten and just automatically took my arm. With her, I didn't feel handicapped. I didn't feel ninety. The gesture just *was*.

About halfway through the film, I couldn't believe my eyes when I saw Brad walk in. It just wasn't his kind of movie. In fact, he'd made it crystal clear that he hated anything captioned and most things foreign. And yet he was here. I'd recognize his perfect profile anywhere.

Then I saw his date and felt my hackles rise. Without thinking, I poked Steph.

"Huh?" I think she finally said. She was engrossed in the film. The people on the screen were eating ribs at an outdoor banquet as though there were no tomorrow.

There was a sudden crescendo of music, and I leaned close to her ear. "Brad," I said, pointing to a spot two rows ahead of us. "And Kari."

"Twerps," she said into my good ear. "Want to leave?"

"No, it's okay, but when the film ends, let's get out of here before they see us." I didn't want them calling me Boozy Beth as I struggled up the aisle.

Steph made the universal "okay" gesture. Then she went back to watching the greasy banquet.

Brad . . . and Kari. I could see between the two pair of shoulders in front of me. Brad's arm was on Kari's shoulder, and they were sitting very close. I forgot the film as I wondered who had moved in on whom.

I was lost in thought when I felt Steph tap my arm. She motioned toward the aisle. With her help, we made it up and out as the movie was winding down. The two lovebirds were nowhere in sight.

"Vultures!" I said when we were outside.

"What?"

"Brad and Kari."

"I thought you were through with him."

"I am. But they're like vultures picking my bones clean. I mean, we're hardly broken up, and they looked like Velcro bunnies."

"You're jealous. You must still have it for him."

Did I? Whatever it was, I didn't want my feelings to spoil this night with my best friend. I shoved it away as we walked to a hamburger place just up the street. Fortunately, it was well-lit and fairly flat, so walking wasn't a nightmare, but there was a maddening hum from traffic that sometimes drowned out Steph's voice. No matter, she was Steph, and she didn't mind repeating.

"Do they still have that special with the mustard sauce?" she asked.

"Yep."

"Oh, great. I'm starved, aren't you?"

And the funny thing was, suddenly I could have eaten a horse.

"Ash and Karen are supposed to meet us," I mentioned as we walked in. It was pretty crowded, but I was relieved to spot them in a booth. Booths could be quieter than some of the tables. They waved at us, and Steph ran over to give them each a hug.

As good as it was to be together, I felt pretty left out. Steph and I had had some time to talk privately, so the part about her and the other two talking a lot didn't matter. But it mattered that I couldn't follow their conversation. There were at least a dozen other conversations going on at other booths and tables. There was some background music. There was the clatter of dishes from the nearby kitchen. Steph sat across the table from me next to Karen, while Ashley was next to me, but even when Ash talked into my good ear, lots of the time I couldn't separate the hodgepodge of sounds and draw out words.

Every once in a while I got a word or phrase from my friends, so I tried to fill in the gaps.

"Ryan . . . ." That was Steph, of course.

"You didn't!" Karen commenting on something.

" . . . a purple sweater if . . . an 'A' . . . ." Karen again.

Ashley was the quietest of our old quartet. She nudged me, and I realized she had asked me something.

"I was daydreaming," I told her.

"I'm sorry about Brad," she repeated.

Everyone must know we'd broken up.

"That's all right," I told her. "I'm over him."

"Good, because here he comes with Kari."

I thought of them loving it up in the theater. Jealous? No, I wasn't jealous, but it did matter that he'd thrown me aside so casually. And it did matter that Kari was the one on his arm now. Boy, did she look smug when she spotted us. *That's right, Kari, flaunt it.* It was just soooo like her that I wanted to puke.

I just shrugged in answer to Ashley's comment, but Steph picked up on it. I knew we'd be talking about it later.

Brad and Kari actually walked up to our table. Although Kari and Steph didn't really know each other, Brad and Steph did, so he made a big thing about coming up to her and acting as though she were his long-lost friend. He said something I missed. Kari, meanwhile, hung on his arm like a leech the whole time.

I was glad when they finally took a table out of my sight. Even so, my hamburger tasted like the horse I thought I'd been hungry for, and I was glad when we got out of there.

Back in my room, Steph said, "I can't believe those two."

"You mean Ash and Karen?"

"Oh no, not them. Brad and Kari. The way she was hanging all over him was awful. I could see them at their table. But what got me, Beth, what I don't understand, is her weird comment."

"Why? What did she say?"

"She said something about booze in your cola. What did she mean?"

"Did I forget to tell you that part earlier tonight?"

"You sure did. Tell me now."

"Kari has given me a nickname, Steph. I guess because of my balance, she's taken to calling me Boozy

Beth. I guess to her I look like a drunk."

I could see the shock on her face.

"That's cruel, Beth. Have you said anything to your dad about it?"

"No. I decided it would just make things worse, but if it gets too bad with Kari, I may have to. I'm just so sick of her."

"Yes, well, I don't know where she's coming from, either. Maybe she's jealous. I mean, if her folks got divorced when she was only a couple of years old, maybe she was used to having her mom all to herself."

"Maybe that's it, partly, but I don't spend much time with Susan. I don't see how Kari could see me as a threat."

"It's hard to get into the mind of another person."

"You can say that again!"

When we finally turned off the lights, we were pretty well talked out, and as I fell asleep, instead of thinking about Brad and Kari, I was remembering a much younger Steph. On her first sleepover, when she was only in kindergarten, she had slept with Gladys, her toy goose. I think I fell asleep smiling at the memory.

Chapter Eight

"Sit down," Mom said one day after school. I could tell from the bandanna covering her hair that she'd been pre-cleaning before the cleaning lady's twice-monthly visit. It might have seemed weird, but the popularity of *Oregon This Morning* made Mom a public figure of sorts, and it just wouldn't do to have a maid going around saying that Toni Langford, the celebrity, had a messy house. I often helped her spruce things up a little.

Today she was just sitting in a wing chair with a feather duster in her hand. Something was wrong. She couldn't have changed her mind about Egypt, could she? Maybe she'd found out Susan wanted to take me shopping. Yeah, that must be it.

"Hi, Mom," I told her. I sat in the matching wing chair. When I looked at Mom again, I realized it must not be the clothes thing. That might have made her mad but not sad.

"What's wrong?" I asked.

"Well, maybe nothing too serious," she told me. "Beth, Granmary was rushed to the hospital this morning."

"Oh no! What's wrong? Is she okay?"

"You know how tired she'd seemed lately."

"And she was having so much trouble getting her breath," I added. Mom nodded.

"They think it's congestive heart failure."

Failure! My hand went over my mouth. We couldn't lose Granmary!

"Oh Mom, that doesn't mean—"

"Not necessarily, honey. The doctors have drained off several pounds of fluid, and she feels better already. Oh Beth, you won't believe it, but even from her hospital bed, she was thinking of you. She called me and wanted me to let you know not to stop by her house tomorrow. She was afraid you would worry if you went over for tea and found an empty house."

I was crying then. It was Granmary through and through to be so thoughtful.

"Can I visit her?" I finally asked as I wiped away my tears. Mom's eyes were misty, too, I saw, and I thought again how nice it was that Mom and Granmary had hit it off so well.

"We'll have to see how things go. I have the number of her room, and we will phone to check up on her progress. For now, how would you like me to call a florist and have an arrangement sent in your name?"

"Yours too, Mom." Having decided upon a spring bouquet, Mom made the call. Then we went into the nook, where I had some milk while she poured herself a cup of coffee.

"Honey, remember, no matter what happens, Granmary is eighty-nine years old. Her system isn't as strong as yours or mine. We have to be prepared, a little, for whatever happens. Mary Sealy," she went on, "has probably crammed three lifetimes into one, don't you think?"

"Oh, yes!" I told her emphatically. Granmary celebrated life.

As awful as Kari had been to me, of course I said something to her at school about Granmary.

"Kari," I told her after French the next day, "I'm sorry Granmary is in the hospital. How's she doing?"

I didn't expect her reaction.

"What's it to you?" she asked, flipping her hair.

"Come on, you know I've grown close to her." In fact, it was I who stopped by for tea, not her own great-granddaughter. Granmary, being Granmary, had made excuses for Kari. She had a busy life with sports. She needed to help her mother, etc. . . . etc. But if I could manage the time, Kari could too. I didn't buy the excuses.

"Yeah, you even wheedled that ring out of her. I know what you're after, Beth Langford."

She started walking away, but I couldn't let her ugly accusation pass. I grabbed her arm, stopping her. When she yanked it out of my grasp, the motion almost toppled me over. Fortunately, a wall was behind me and I leaned back into it without falling.

"Kari, that's a horrible thing to imply. I love her. The only thing I've been after, as you put it, is her good company."

"Hide your real motive if you want, but just remember that she's my family, not yours."

"Mesdemoiselles!" I suddenly heard. Miss Latham, looking sort of stern, was coming back into the room. She rattled off something in very fast French. I didn't know what it was, but it looked like a scolding.

"Excusez-moi!" I told her, ashamed that Kari and I had made a mini-scene.

"Et moi," Kari added.

Shaken by the whole thing, I didn't even look at Kari again. We smiled at Miss Latham and then went our separate ways.

That brat! I was only trying to be decent. To think I had to see her again that day turned my stomach.

When Susan picked me up after school, I was sure the shopping trip for Egypt clothes would be out, what with Granmary's trouble. Since I didn't have the heart for it, it didn't matter anyway. Now I wanted to go even less, with Kari so recently awful. But Susan still wanted to go.

"Granmary wants us to," she assured me. "At first I told her no in no uncertain terms. But you know Granmary. She told me she'd be furious if we didn't have something to tell her about clothes the next time we get together. So . . . ."

"That really sounds like her," I said, but something caught in my voice.

Susan reached out her hand and touched mine reassuringly. Her warm brown eyes met mine as she said, "We have to hope for the best, Beth."

"I know, Susan." We were still at the curb, and as if Susan just realized that, she finally turned the ignition back on.

"Where's Kari?" I asked as Susan started to drive away.

"I forgot she had an appointment for an allergy shot this afternoon. She's going to join us afterward, but you and I can get started."

Hooray! A reprieve, I thought.

"How is Granmary today?" I asked on the way.

"Pretty good, considering, Beth. She can breathe a lot more easily now that the fluid's off, for one thing, but she's getting some antibiotics to guard against infection, and they're making her feel nauseated. She didn't feel much like company today. Would you like to visit her with us tomorrow?"

I really didn't want to, not with Kari after what she'd said. Still, it was nice of Susan to ask me along.

"Thanks for asking. Susan, would you mind if Mom and I went together on our own?"

"Not at all," she told me, and once again, I was surprised at how decent she could be if Mom's name came up. It certainly didn't work that way in reverse, I thought, as I remembered Mom's repeated references to Susan as "that woman," as if she had fangs and bright red horns.

On principle, I'd despised Susan at first. Then I realized that I'd only hated the reality of Mom and Dad's split. I wasn't ever supposed to have a *step*mother, was

I? But Susan had been nice to me, and I'd grown to like her, if not her bratty daughter, in spite of the bad situation.

Now, as we neared Washington Square, a big shopping mall, Susan said, "By the way, Granmary appreciates the beautiful flowers you and your mother sent. Irises are her favorites."

"Good," I told her.

"I was going to start at Nordstrom's," she said as she pulled her compact car into a parking slot, "but your dad thought of a store in the mall that specializes in rugged clothes. Granmary said we may also have to make a trip to that big outdoor outfitters for things like the right kind of hat."

"Yeah. You need a really good one, I've heard. Even March can be scorching there." I thought again of feeling the heat of the desert sand through my shoes. I must have smiled.

"You're really looking forward to the trip, aren't you?"

"You know it!"

Susan hadn't had experience with me in a mall. I think she was sort of surprised to find out the way my hearing conked out, thanks to too many background distractions, and that I needed to walk along the very edge of an aisle to keep from getting bumped.

We couldn't talk much as we walked along the mall's wide, people-crammed halls.

Inside the store, it was quieter. She watched me walk over to my size.

"I'm not used to such little clothes," she told me. I knew what she meant. She and Kari were both 5'9" or so to my 5'2".

Mom had already taken me shopping, but the more I looked at the clothes before me now, the more I realized that Mom's idea of "Egypt wear," as she called it, was a little too put-together and dressy. To please Mom, I would wear one of her outfits on the plane, though, and they'd also be great for church and stuff.

"These look perfect," Susan said as she pulled out a pair of khakis with lots of little pockets. I nodded.

"I like these shirts," I told her. They were camp shirts in lots of different colors.

"With all the pockets, we won't have to bother with purses," she told me.

When we tried the clothes on, though, my heart sank as it usually did when I tried things on. Nothing ever fit right. Even though I weighed under 100 pounds, my chest and hips filled things out when the rest of me didn't. In the mirror, I looked like I had on my big sister's clothes. The pants were too long and much too big in the waist, but I knew I wouldn't be able to squeeze my stupid hips into the next smaller size. Well, Zelda could alter them, I guessed. Fortunately, she was able to get around a little.

Susan's pants fit perfectly, but we laughed at each other when we came out of our dressing rooms.

"We look like bwanas or something, don't we?" I commented. She had on a cream-colored camp shirt with her pants. My shirt was gold. "Here," I told her, handing her a jacket with a zillion more little pockets. She put it on. Laughing at herself, she said, "Now I really look like I'm going on safari."

"We certainly do," I answered as I slipped on a similar jacket. The sleeves managed to hang down way too far.

"Do they have a shorter size for you?" she asked. When we searched but didn't find anything, I explained about Zelda.

"Well then, why don't we take these in both the tan and that ugly olive color?"

"Ick," I said.

"I couldn't agree more."

"But going purseless would be handy."

"Exactly," we both said at the same time.

We didn't find hats, but with our slacks and the lightweight jackets to shield us from the sun, we were getting in pretty good shape. We bought them and set some aside for Kari's approval.

"Granmary will be so tickled," Susan said.

"I can hardly wait to tell her," I seconded.

"Let's have something cool to drink," Susan suggested.

"Shopping is such hard work," I laughed.

We walked down about half the length of the mall and took the escalator up to the food court, where Kari was supposed to meet us, Susan said.

As we had our drinks, we talked. Or maybe I should say tried to talk. The buzz of background conversations and other noises really messed up my hearing aid reception, and the food court was one of those places with a high ceiling and big open space that just made all that sound sort of bounce around and get lost.

Before I could even explain to Susan, she picked right up on it. She said something up close to my ear. Unfortunately, it was the dead ear.

"Let me sit on the other side," I told her.

"I'm sorry," she apologized.

"Oh, that's okay. People forget which one it is with my hair covering it and all."

"It must be hard to hear in a place like this."

"Yeah, it can be. Susan, I'll probably have to ask you to repeat things, but I'd rather talk than just sit here."

"Me, too."

She did have to repeat a lot, but she seemed so patient that my estimation of my new stepmother went up a notch.

As we sipped our drinks, I commented, "It must have been fun growing up around Granmary."

"Oh, it was, Beth," she told me. I pieced together her words as she went on. "She always fed our imaginations. I remember when I wanted to play bride, she always had a piece of lace for me to wear as a veil, or when I wanted to learn to ride a horse, it was Granmary who gamely went along even though I found out later that riding was one of her few real fears."

I heard her say Kari's name and knew I wanted to get that part just right.

"What?" I asked.

"Oh, I just said that it's too bad Kari has missed out on that," she repeated.

"Missed out? How?"

"Oh, nothing in particular. She just doesn't like to go over to visit much. I could force her, but my grandmother is a sharp cookie, Beth. She doesn't want people there out of duty, and I'm sorry to say that Kari might make her feel that way. I don't really understand it, either, because Kari loved going when she was little."

I couldn't think of anything to say to that.

"The odd thing is, Kari volunteers as a reader to older people in a hospice."

That was news to me. Kari?

Susan steered the conversation toward me.

"Thanks so much for your time with Granmary, Beth. I can't tell you how much she enjoys it."

"It works both ways. I really like being with her."

"I'm so glad you're going to Egypt with us."

"Me, too. It's going to be a great trip."

"Oh look," she said, motioning toward the escalator at the far end of the food court, "there's Kari and her ride."

Why couldn't she just have gotten lost on the way? I felt even more strongly about it when I saw her "ride."

"Hello, ladies," Brad told Susan and me as they strolled up to our table.

"Hi," Kari said, all smiles. You'd never guess she had been such a witch after French class. I could tell she was just trying to flaunt being with my old boyfriend. The funny thing was, it actually hurt to see them together.

Susan and I greeted them.

"Why don't you have a drink with us before we go to the store?" When they nodded, Susan added, "Kari, come with me to get the drinks, and I can fill you in on the clothes I had set aside for you to look at. You don't mind, Brad, do you?"

Go home, Brad, I wanted to say, but he just shook his head.

When Susan and Kari had gone, Brad looked at me for a long time.

"I miss you," he told me. He spoke into my good ear. His voice was easier to hear than Susan's higher-pitched one. "Can we talk?"

"We are talking."

"That's not what I meant."

"We broke up," I reminded him.

"I know, Beth. I'm not asking you out. I'm just asking if we can talk."

Susan and Kari were coming back.

"Okay, Brad. Meet me in my yard by that bench before school tomorrow morning."

He nodded just as they sat back down. After making small talk with Susan and slurping his orange soda, he started to leave. Kari gushed something at him as she reached for his hand and gave it a sickening squeeze. Was it for my benefit, or were they really that tight already?

After he was gone, Kari finished her drink. Then

she started rubbing in the fact that she was still playing tennis often with my dad. I almost wished my hearing aid battery would die.

"I don't know if you know, Beth," she said ever-so-sweetly, "but Bruce and I are going to play in a father-daughter tournament in two weeks. We've been practicing like mad and think we have a good chance to win. We're so great together."

Susan smiled, totally missing the undercurrents.

A father-daughter tournament? As I remembered the curtsey fiasco and Dad's pressure over the years to try to turn me into something I wasn't, I felt sort of sick. Did my father think of Kari Quinn as a bundle of fun? Was she the normal daughter he'd always wanted?

I was so tired of feeling hurt that I had to do something. Kari would get hers.

Chapter Nine

Brad was sitting on the old stone bench in my yard the next morning when I walked out.

"How long have you been here?" I asked. It was a chilly morning.

"Not long. Here," he motioned, "sit down."

"I still don't think we have anything to talk about."

"Let's find out," he said. "Beth, I was stupid to do what I did in the family room. But at least let me explain. Do you remember that I asked you if I could show you how much I care?"

I nodded.

"Well, I meant one thing and you thought I meant another. See, I'm a guy, and I don't think we always see things the way you do. You think in terms of romance, and guys my age . . . well . . . it's just natural for a guy to want to hold his girl and feel her warmth next to him. Look at yourself in the mirror, Beth. You're very . . . very . . . holdable."

"I don't know if that's a compliment or not," I told him. *Holdable?*

"Believe me," he said with feeling, "it is. But I apologize for trying if that's not what you wanted too."

His apology after all this time surprised me.

"I accept your apology. In fact, I want to apologize, too, if I gave you mixed signals. I thought you knew that I want to wait for some things.

"But Brad, how could you have gone straight from us to Kari, if you cared so much for me?"

He hung his head so low that I couldn't help feeling sorry for him. He finally looked up, but his eyes

. . . .
83

met mine and then darted away.

"I know I botched it. I felt so rejected, and Kari was just there, you know."

"Is she 'holdable' too?" I couldn't help asking.

"That's not very nice, Beth."

"Well, is she?" I persisted.

"She's not you," he said, reaching for my hand. "You're just very special to me."

"Special? Then why did you call me Boozy Beth?" I asked as the sudden memory brought back a wave of terrible hurt. "Don't you have any idea how much that hurt?"

"I'll say it again," he told me. "I felt rejected, embarrassed, maybe even humiliated."

"Humiliated? Brad, how do you think it felt on those stairs when I fell and people, including your current girlfriend, laughed at me? How do you think it feels not to walk right and be called names for something I can't even help? I don't drink anything stronger than cola and, sometimes, coffee or tea. No," I corrected, "since it's a time for honesty, I'll take that back. I did have a glass of champagne at Dad and Susan's wedding reception. But you know I don't drink. Boozy Beth. Boozy Beth? What am I, some kind of circus act? *You* felt humiliated!"

I got off the bench. This conversation was pointless. And then something he said stopped me in my tracks.

"I was humiliated when you started hanging out with my brother. You've always loved him, haven't you? If he held you, you wouldn't pull away, would you? Oh no, Beth, humiliation works two ways. I've tried to apologize. If you ever see beyond the nose on your face, let me know."

Then he walked away.

Stunned, I sat back down. "Hanging out" with

Matt? Wasn't it just like Brad to exaggerate like that? And yet wasn't Matt my standard for all guys, including Brad?

I didn't have time to examine the rest of that conversation before school. Matt was pulling into the driveway.

He noticed that I was sort of quiet on the way to school.

"I'm just worried about Granmary," I told him, which was certainly true. I just didn't fill him in on the rest.

"How's she doing, Beth?" he asked. Although Matt knew her mainly from the things I'd said, he had finally met her just days before her collapse, when I'd taken him with me for tea.

"Oh, so-so, I'd say. Mom and I are going to visit her at the hospital tomorrow. She's not feeling so hot right now from the medications they're giving her."

"I'm sorry to hear that." He thought awhile and then shifted conversational gears by saying, "I hope you won't think I'm trying to minimize her illness, but I have a surprise for you. Can you meet me at my car after school?"

"A surprise?" I asked with raised eyebrows. "I guess so." I looked at him sideways.

"No! No hints," he said, reading my look correctly. "And by the way, I mentioned this to your mother so that she won't worry if you're a little late."

Just like Matt, I thought.

In a way, Kari ignored me all day at school, but in another way, she spoke volumes. She was hanging all over Brad like a mink stole, for one thing. And then I found an anonymous newspaper clipping on alcoholism in teens taped onto my locker. Kari, I guessed. In red pen, certain things were underlined, including loss of balance.

···············
85

With Matt's surprise a big question mark all day, my classes seemed to drag as my curiosity grew. When I walked past him in the hall at one point, he only winked at me. The mystery was still on when I met him at his car after my last class.

"Where are we going?" I asked as we headed toward Portland.

"You'll see," he answered playfully. "It isn't too far."

Right on the edge of the city limits, we stopped at an old Victorian house.

"Curiouser and curiouser," I told him as we walked up the stairs. Not only didn't Matt knock, but when he pulled out a key and turned it in the lock and the door opened, I said, "Your new apartment. Oh, this is a neat house."

The big, glass-fronted door eased open, and he flicked on the lights.

"Nope," he said. "Guess again."

The room in front of me looked like a big living room with a hardwood floor, but it was almost empty of any furniture, and it had mirrors along one wall and a *barre*.

"It's a dance studio," I said.

"That it is."

"I don't understand, Matt."

"Just bear with me," he said as he walked over to the edge of the room. He opened a cupboard, and when he turned around, I saw the dress of my dreams.

It was layer upon layer of the floatiest chiffon, in purest white, and there were ostrich feathers around the hem of the skirt.

"Here," he told me, "put this on while I change, too." He pointed to what must be a dressing room.

"But Matt, I can't—"

"Shh."

....
86

A dancing dress? Botched ballet lessons flitted before me. But this was Matt, and when I looked into his dark eyes, a current of trust passed between us. It wouldn't hurt to humor him, I decided, and it'd be fun to see how I looked in such a beautiful gown.

"Okay. Be right back," I told him as I carefully carried the dress with me.

"Take these too," Matt said as he handed me the paper bag. Inside were my low-heeled white pumps. Mom, I thought.

I was so used to seeing myself in jeans and sweaters that I laughed out loud when I saw my reflection in the mirror. And yet I looked . . . well . . . I looked pretty, like a woman. The cut of the dress accentuated my small waist, concealed my big hips and showed off my bustline in a way that didn't make it look like a silly ledge. The pure white was perfect with my near-black hair, and my curls didn't even look poodle-y. They suddenly seemed romantic and just right. I reached into my purse and pulled out a lipstick in a shade a little darker than I usually wore to school. I put it on and brushed on some fresh blush.

Dressed for disaster, I thought.

When I came out of the dressing room, Matt was already waiting, in a black tux with tails. He looked at me in a brand new way, smiled, and bowed deeply.

"May I have this dance?" he asked, holding out his hand.

Without thinking, I took it. For a moment, I imagined us gliding across the floor like Fred and Ginger, our feet in perfect harmony with the music and each other. But the beautiful vision suddenly faded as reality hit.

I pulled my hand away.

"This is so sweet, Matt, but I can't dance."

"Beth, I'm not your father. This won't be like the

curtsey or ballet or tennis. You don't have to meet anybody's standards."

"But my balance."

"I know. And maybe your balance would prohibit your dancing in a roomful of other dancers. But this is just us, Beth. No one is here to bump us. There's no chatter to interfere with the sound of the music. And most of all, I won't let you fall. I don't expect you to be perfect."

"I don't know, Matt. You know I tried ballet. I was awfully clumsy, and it really hurt not to keep up with the rest of the class."

"I can understand that. But 'keeping up with the rest of the class' is the problem. Maybe you can't physically do that. Maybe you can't physically get your balance mechanism to do what you want it to. But it's the feeling. If dancing is beautiful in your heart, then it is beautiful even if you stumble a little."

"And you say you know the steps."

"Well, that's true. I've watched them so many times on the ballroom dancing championships on television, and I've practiced them in my room. I've just never had someone to dance that way with."

"Until now." He walked over to the CD changer and put on a disc.

Emperor Waltz.

"May I have this dance?" he asked again.

"You may," I told him this time.

And then we were dancing. *Dancing!* We were Fred and Ginger. Our steps were very precise, but when my balance made me stumble, he was there to hold me up, and when I had to move more slowly than the music called for, he slowed to my pace. It would have been disaster with other people moving to the right tempo on the floor, whirling, maybe bumping, but as Matt had said, this was just us.

I was living in a dream, dancing a Viennese waltz with a handsome man with whom I felt as a single unit. I knew I was supposed to follow him, but because I never knew which little turn might topple me slightly, he followed me, and it was like there was no balance problem at all. There was no concentrating, concentrating, concentrating, in a step-by-step approach, as I used with the stairs at school. I was free to glide, and I don't think I'd ever been happier in my life.

When the music ended, he didn't say anything except, "Let's try one more." He moved back to the CD player and put on a new disc.

The room had a good sound system, but this time the music started so softly that at first I guess I didn't hear it. He picked up on it.

"You'll hear it in a moment," Matt told me.

And then I did. It was only the music and not the words, but I had heard it clearly at home, since Mom liked the song, and I'd memorized the words.

"I hear it now," I said. Then I was back in Matt's arms, dancing slowly.

In my mind, Matt sang to me as the melody wafted hauntingly into my good ear:

> Unforgettable, that's what you are,
> Unforgettable, tho' near or far—

I stumbled then, but Matt's strong arms kept me from falling, and even though it could have been the opposite of romantic, he turned it into part of the song somehow by not making me feel clumsy.

It was a different experience altogether from the Viennese waltz. Instead of being my dancing fantasy, it was a dream come true of another kind. I was in Matt's arms, close, and I smelled the faint scent of his morning soap and shampoo. We weren't Fred and Ginger now.

We were Matt and Beth. And I was glad.

I'd missed a line or two of words in my mind, but now they continued:

> Never before has someone been more
> Unforgettable in ev'ry way,
> And forevermore,
> That's how you'll stay.
> That's why, darling, it's incredible,
> That someone so unforgettable
> Thinks that I am unforgettable, too.

When the song was over, he held me to him, I thought, for a moment or two longer than the music lasted.

"Thank you, Matt," I told him as we broke apart. "What a perfect surprise. How did you ever think of it?"

"You inspired me. Remember when you mentioned dancing one day on the way to school? Well, I just filed it away and decided to act on it. It's time a dream or two came true."

"How did you know which music to choose?"

"You inspired that, too. I thought of the old Fred-and-Ginger routines from their movies. You know, when they danced to the *Carioca* and *Cheek to Cheek,* but do you know why I didn't pick them?"

I could guess.

"The footwork is too fancy and fast for me," he said, and I broke out laughing.

"It was fun being a Viennese lady. I'm ready to be Beth again," I said. "Shall we change?"

"I guess so, but I'll always remember you in that dress."

"I hate to take it off."

"You have to," he told me, "but you don't have to leave it here. It's a gift from me to you."

For a few seconds, I stared at him in disbelief. Then I hugged him before going to change.

My room looked so normal that night, with its yellow walls, blue carpet, and blue-and-yellow comforter and pillows. As I lay back against the pillows, I looked at the beautiful gown hanging from a hook on my closet door. In my mind, briefly, I was dancing again to the *Emperor Waltz,* feeling the wonderful dream coming true. That fantasy was safe.

The other one wasn't.

You've always loved him, haven't you? Brad's voice of that morning echoed in my mind. *If he held you, you wouldn't pull away, would you?*

Matt.

He was everything I wanted in a man. He was kind, sensitive, fun to be with, intelligent. Brad might be the handsomer of the two, but it was Matt's crooked nose and his funny, little-boy cowlick that touched my heart. How could anyone else ever have thought up the day's wonderful surprise? How could anyone else have known how to make dancing—probably the bane of my existence—seem so right? Who else would have stumbled on purpose, so gracefully, just to be in harmony with me? No more Boozy Beth. No more wishing some guy could be more like Matt. He was Matt.

Yes, I had to admit I'd probably always loved Matt, in a nice, safe way. But now I was in love with him, too. It was, at the same time, the most momentous, wondrous realization, but also the most heartbreaking.

He was twenty-three to my almost-sixteen.

Chapter Ten

When he picked me up the following morning, everything was the same, and yet not the same. It wasn't that we had crossed any lines with anything we had done. It was a "feelings" thing on my part. He looked as he'd looked yesterday, I trusted with the same trust, and I valued our conversations as much as always.

But there was that knowledge that I was in love, and it was bittersweet. I couldn't let him know.

He smiled as I opened the door. I wanted to take the smile and put it in my pocket and keep it there to look at over and over, all day long.

I smiled back and climbed in.

"Thank you again for that wonderful surprise: the dancing, the dress, the feeling of . . . of realizing a dream I was sure would never come true."

"Some dreams are meant to," he told me as he patted my hand. Did he leave his hand over mine a moment longer than he needed to, or was it my imagination? I was glad he didn't make a joke of it and call me Ginger or anything. I may have been Ginger in my mind for a time, but the real dream was dancing as myself. "I enjoyed it as much as you did," he added.

That made my heart sing.

Then we were back to normal, talking about other kinds of things, like Egypt and his teaching.

"I have a student whose IEP doesn't seem to fit," he told me after I'd described the big Temple of Hatshepsut that was one of Granmary's must-sees.

"IEP?"

"Individual Education Plan. Each of the special ed students is required by law to have one as sort of a master plan to make the most of his or her education."

"I thought they just took what we did."

"Well, they do, but the emphasis here is upon individualized education that maximizes their strengths and addresses their weaknesses. They're all tested as a step in determining their IEP. The deaf kids I've been working with tend to need some remedial work with English, reading, and speech, so their IEPs incorporate time for such work.

"Which is where Josh comes into the picture. Josh," he explained, "had meningitis at fourteen. He has very powerful hearing aids and gets a little sound, but for all practical purposes, he's totally deaf. Josh's fourteen years of normal hearing should have given him a very solid English language base, but he tested low. I've been watching Josh and think he's better than he tested."

"Do you think the tests were wrong?" I asked. Poor Josh.

"Not necessarily, but do you know what I think?" he asked. I caught the enthusiasm in his voice and was touched by his interest in his students.

"No, what?"

"I think everyone's overlooking the etiology, or cause, of his deafness. Meningitis is one of those diseases that can cause other problems. I've been doing a little reading on it and ran across a case study of a girl who sounds a lot like Josh. For some reason, her brain couldn't think in certain ways for a year or so after her illness. She couldn't use her imagination or see some of the themes in literature, for instance, whereas that had been a strength for her before getting sick. She only lost certain abilities temporarily. They came back to her in time, and I think I'm seeing this in Josh."

"Wow. That could really mess up his learning. Josh is lucky to have you rooting for him. What are you going to do?"

"There isn't too much I can do. I'm only a student myself, you know. But I plan to talk to my cooperating teacher. Maybe she can do something."

"Good luck," I told him. When he nodded, I changed the subject.

"Mom and I were going to visit Granmary at the hospital today, but they want us to wait a couple more days."

"Is she doing any better?" he asked.

"A little," I told him as the sprawl of the school came into view. "We're here."

"See you tomorrow, if not before," he told me.

"Okay. Again, good luck with the Josh thing."

"Have a nice day," he told me as he pulled away. I liked the way he usually let me out in front, because the parking lot could be a madhouse right before school started, and dodging cars and people wasn't easy for me.

I had the books I needed for morning classes with me, but since I wanted to drop off my jacket, I stopped at my locker on my way into the building. Taped to it was a caricature of a big-busted, floozy-looking woman with dark curls drinking out of a bottle. The artwork was labeled "Boozy Beth" and no doubt meant just for me. I felt like dying when I thought of how many people must have already walked past my locker and seen it. Not only was it a cruel mockery of my balance, but something like that could start rumors that I drank.

Kari. It had to be Kari Quinn who had done this. It was the last straw.

I don't know exactly when during the day the plan started taking shape in my mind. Maybe it had been worming its way into my consciousness for a long time. I only knew I'd had it with her awfulness. During a study period, I ticked it off on a sheet of paper:

1. Kari laughing at my fall on the stairs
2. Kari calling me names
3. Kari accusing me of being after her great-grandmother's things
4. Kari messing with my reputation
5. Kari moving in on my dad
6. Kari showing off with my ex-boyfriend.

When I got to this last point, a little lightbulb went on. Wouldn't it serve her right if I took Brad away from her? Brad missed me, he'd said. If I ever saw beyond the nose on my face, I was supposed to let him know, he'd also told me. Yes, it might work.

I called Brad that night.

"Hello." Matt. I almost hung up.

"Oh, Matt, this is Beth. Could I talk to Brad?"

"Brad? What do you want with him?"

Oh, Matt, it's you I want to talk to, you I want to be with, you I love, I wanted to say.

"I wanted to ask him something about the Blazers," I said lamely.

"Let me put him on," I heard Matt say. Did he sound disappointed?

"Yeah?" I heard after a few seconds. "Beth? Matt said you wanted me."

"I have a couple of Blazers tickets," I told him, "and I thought you might want to go."

"Like to? I'd love to," he said without hesitation. "You know how great it is to watch them in person."

I did know how crazy he was about his Trailblazers. In fact, our mutual love of them was the part of our friendship that I really missed. And going with Brad, with lots of people around, would be safe.

"When?" he asked.

Here it came.

"The fourteenth," I told him. "They're playing

Seattle."

"Sounds perfect. I'll be in touch about picking you up for the game."

Then the call was over.

Hooray! He'd fallen for it. The fourteenth just happened to be Valentine's Day, a day I was sure Kari would like to spend with him. She'd have kittens when he went to a basketball game—with me—instead.

Mom had gotten two tickets from someone at work. Aware of my break-up with Brad, she didn't want me to spend Valentine's Day in my room, so she'd gotten them as a treat for me even though she hated the sport. When I'd asked earlier if she'd mind if I went with a friend, she hadn't at all. In fact, she confessed that she had turned down a date. A guest on the show had asked her out. By the way she blushed, I knew she wasn't sacrificing anything by not going to a ballgame. "Bill" had told her if she changed her mind, the invitation would still be open.

Was Mom interested in someone? Boy, that would be great, because then maybe she'd finally be happier again and even start being more civil about Dad. I just hoped that if it turned into anything, *he* wouldn't have any bratty daughters. One stepsister was one too many, as far as I was concerned.

Matt wasn't very happy when he picked me up the morning after the phone call, and I wasn't either.

"How did things go with Josh's IEP?" I asked.

"He's going to be retested," he said in a dull voice.

"That's great."

The conversation kept going back and forth in tiny sentences for awhile. Then he asked, "What's going on?"

"What do you mean?"

"With Brad."

Matt was too old for me, and Brad was just the right age. Wouldn't it be better just to try to patch things up with Brad and push Matt into some corner of my mind? And maybe if Matt thought I was back with Brad, he'd never know he was the one I loved. But a kaleidoscope of memories of both brothers burst to light in my mind, and I knew I had to be honest with Matt.

"It's not what it seems like," I told him. "I asked Brad to a Blazers game."

"I thought you two were through."

"Well, we are, as far as I'm concerned. I know that seems like a contradiction, but can't we just let it go at that?"

"If you want to let it go."

But suddenly I didn't want to let it go at all.

"Okay, it probably sounds crazy, but I asked him because I can't stand the way my stepsister treats me." Matt, who knew about a few of Kari's pranks, nodded. "It's not like it's unfair to Brad, really. I mean, he loves the live games, and he didn't have to agree to go."

"That's true," Matt agreed. I could tell he was leaving something unsaid.

"But?" I asked.

"Be careful about playing games, Beth. They can backfire."

Granmary looked so fragile in her hospital bed when Mom and I went to visit her after school the next day. She was sleeping. Mom and I were about to tiptoe back out into the hallway, but Granmary either heard or sensed us. Her eyelids fluttered.

"Kari, is that you?" she asked in a weak voice with so much hope that it broke my heart. For just a moment when she opened her eyes, I saw disappointment cloud them. Then it was gone.

"Toni. Beth." she said warmly. I could barely hear her, so I moved a little closer.

"How are you feeling today?" Mom asked as she kissed the older woman's forehead. I only blew her one, but she liked that and blew one back.

"I've felt more chipper," Granmary laughed lightly.

"I've missed our teas," I told her.

"Oh, that's sweet, dear. I have, too, and we shall take them up again soon." Then to both of us she said, "Thank you for the lovely bouquet. It's usually the first thing I see when I open my eyes." I missed words here and there, but when she pointed to the flowers, it sort of fell together. The irises, her favorites according to Susan, were wilting a little, but the daffodils and other spring flowers still looked perfect.

Granmary wanted company but couldn't talk too much herself without getting tired, so she asked us to do the talking. Mom and I chatted about the weather, clothes for Egypt (Mom, maybe because of Granmary's being in the hospital, hadn't even laid into me about the shopping trip with Susan), and Mom's guests of the week for *Oregon This Morning.*

Then Mom said, "I'm going to go down the hall for a coffee and let you two talk for a bit."

After she left, I told Granmary about Matt and the dancing.

"That's so romantic, Beth," she told me, but she sounded winded.

"Remember," I reminded her, "let me do the talking."

"Oh, pshaw. Come close, Beth," she said, scaring me a little. It was almost as if she had something important to tell me—something she had to say now.

I moved up near her head.

"I'm right here," I told her.

"No matter what happens, you go to Egypt and

see if its magic doesn't affect you. You and Kari, too. And, Beth dear, be true to yourself and follow your heart in all you do. I'm just so tired."

"I know," I told her. I could hear the tiredness. "I'll remember what you said. I'm going to let you rest now."

"Don't you dare," she said with mock sternness. I could hear her now that she was almost talking into my ear. "I'm not finished. Hopefully there will be years more. Just remember that when my life ends, Beth, celebrate. Celebrate my life with smiles, because I've skipped my way along most merrily.

"And now," she pronounced, "I really am tired."

"I will remember every word, Granmary," I assured her. It was time to let her rest even if she protested again. "Mom and I will come back to see you in a few days."

"Do that, dear. 'Bye for now."

"Good-bye, Granmary."

I found Mom just finishing her coffee in the lounge.

"She's really too tired for more company," I explained. "I said good-bye for you."

Mom nodded understandingly and said, "We'll come back."

We had gotten about halfway to the elevator. Since long corridors were murder for me because they knocked out my sense of perspective, I was concentrating on walking without falling when I sensed, rather than saw, Mom tense up.

I slowed my walk and looked up. Susan and Dad were coming toward us from the opposite direction.

Don't make a scene, I silently begged.

As we came almost even with them, Susan said something I didn't hear, but from the way she looked from me to Mom, I thought she'd probably said "hello."

Mom, though, was on my good side. I would have heard her if she'd said anything, and she hadn't said a word. In fact, she cut them dead. I smiled apologetically at Dad and Susan and greeted them as we passed. Susan smiled at me but kept on walking toward Granmary's room. I might have said something about Granmary being so tired, but I just wanted to get Mom into the elevator before Dad said something to set her off.

Dad paused in the hallway. What was he thinking?

Mom walked on and reached the bank of elevators. When one wasn't available, she furiously punched the DOWN button over and over. She was still punching when Dad came up to us.

He said something into my bad ear. Wouldn't he ever get it right?

"What?" I said. I didn't feel like I should always have to turn my good ear toward him, but it was often that way. I did that now.

"I'm looking forward to this weekend," he told me.

"Me, too."

Now go away, Dad, I thought. With Granmary lying in there, now wasn't the time for this. I just knew he'd say something to rile Mom. Would they duke it out in a hospital, of all places?

"Toni," he said, "I'm still waiting for those pictures. I don't want to have to bring in Harry Worden about this." Harry Worden was his lawyer. As much as I wanted Dad to have some photos of me, I was mad at him for bringing it up now.

There was no duking it out. Mom didn't say a word. She didn't even look at him. When the elevator door finally opened, she got in as though he didn't even exist. I got in beside her.

As the door closed, I saw Dad shaking his head,

....
100

and I don't know if I smiled to comfort him or glared in reprimand.

Why did they have to be such babies? Why did they play these games?

Be careful about playing games, Beth. They can backfire. Matt's words.

Was it a game to try to get Brad to go with me to watch the Blazers? True, he wanted to go, but wouldn't that be leading him on? I'd liked watching games with Brad, but what about the rest? I didn't really want to date him again. Oh sure, he was the right age, but was age enough? Hardly.

And yet it would be so sweet to get back at Kari Quinn.

Chapter Eleven

Mom actually did go out with Bill Redeker on Valentine's Day. A widower with a college-age son, he seemed okay, and Mom reminded me of myself getting ready for my first date. Not only did she want my opinion every step of the way about her hair and stuff, but she changed her outfit three times before settling on a little black dress and pearls. I'd meant it when I'd told her she looked really glam.

Of course, if I'd thought a new man in her life would soften her toward Dad, I was way off the mark. Although it didn't make sense to me, she'd just really written him off. I got my hopes up one day, for instance, when I'd seen a big box of pictures Mom was setting aside for Dad. Good, finally this dumb issue would get settled, and it looked as though I wouldn't be in the middle of it again.

Only, one weekend when I was at Dad and Susan's, I had seen Mom's selection of pictures. If it hadn't been so sad and stupid, it might have been funny. Mom must have spent hours going through my baby and little girl pictures and every other picture we'd kept over the years. Dad ended up with the out-of-focus ones of me, the ones of animals at the zoo, and some oldies of him with his high school and college buddies. There were pictures of barns in Iowa and the Empire State Building in New York City. But they weren't what Dad wanted, and Mom knew it.

Talk about games people play!

As for games, I wavered back and forth. Should I go with Brad to the game on Valentine's Day or shouldn't I? Sometimes it seemed okay, but other times it seemed dead wrong. Back and forth I went.

Kari just about decided me in favor of going ahead. She just didn't know when to stop, and I'd just love to see her face when Brad and I went out together again.

Tennis is a case in point. When she and Dad won second-place in the tournament, of course she had lorded it over me: "We were such a strong team. We were perfect partners." *Blah, blah, blah.*

What she didn't know was that I'd snuck in and watched part of their match. Some strange force just made me go. I had to admit they really were great together, but watching them was like picking open a healing scab. That was supposed to be me out there with Dad—it was a father-daughter event, after all—not Kari Quinn. Salt in the wound was the memory of Dad's exasperation at my own tennis bomb-out a few years earlier. "You're not trying hard enough, Beth," he'd said. "Just apply yourself."

Yes, Kari deserved some kind of comeuppance. I would go with Brad. It wasn't as if he didn't want to, was it?

And then I ran across the poem Matt had given me after that episode in the family room with Brad. "Wishing You Were He" it was called. I didn't know who the author was. Hadn't Matt said she was a hearing-impaired girl about my age? Anyway, I'd read the poem then, but it had gotten in with some sketches of zylem and phloem, and I'd totally forgotten about it. Now as I pulled out the diagrams for an upcoming test, a couple of the stanzas jumped right out at me:

> Everywhere I see his face, hear his laugh,
> Wishing that you were he
> Or, maybe, I not me.

Sometimes I feel a little like a fake;
In wishing you were he
I'm stifling what is me.

Brad was wrong for me. Hadn't I always wanted him to be more like Matt, wishing him into a more sensitive, caring, and mature person than he was or, perhaps, would ever be?

I loved Matt, not Brad. In trying to deny my feelings, wasn't I "stifling what is me"? I would have to examine that idea more as time went by, but at least the poem had the effect of making my decision for me about Valentine's Day. I wouldn't play a fakey, stupid game.

Brad went to the Blazers game, instead of to the party at Lia's with Kari, but he went without me. When he didn't even seem put out when I handed him the two tickets and told him to take a friend, I knew he'd never really cared that much for me as a human being in the first place. I was just potentially "holdable" in his eyes. His reaction sort of put a final period to the short chapter that had been our relationship.

Even though I ended up home alone on Valentine's Day, I didn't feel sorry for myself. I mean, I was glad I hadn't gone with him. And the funny thing was, even though I'd come to my senses and decided that getting back at Kari through Brad was wrong, it did put a big dent in their relationship.

Lia's party was a big event, and I wish I could have been a fly on the wall when Brad told Kari he was going to a basketball game instead of the romantic little dinner Ashley had heard Kari talking about, followed by the party at Lia's.

Whether or not Kari knew the tickets had come from me, I didn't know, but her pranks continued. There were the occasional ugly messages on my locker, the name-calling, and her cut-me-dead looks.

But if that hurt, a different, deeper kind was about to happen.

Granmary got to go home from the hospital, but she wasn't very strong, and her niece, Betty, moved in for company and to help out. Susan's parents had died years ago in a small plane crash. In any case, Granmary still enjoyed company, so we had a couple more tea parties together. Then one day Susan called with the terrible news that Betty had found Granmary dead in her room. Her heart had simply given out while she was crocheting.

I felt totally numb. I'd never lost anyone I'd loved before.

"Celebrate my life with smiles," she'd told me, so I tried not to cry. But I missed her achingly. I knew I would miss going to her house, miss the easy way we talked, and miss having her to share my excitement about Egypt with.

Not long after her death, I went into the yard to think about her. The Japanese cherry trees were in full bloom, pinking the Oregon landscape with an early taste of spring. We had three of the beautiful trees behind the house, back near my favorite stone bench.

She would have liked it here, I thought as I watched a few pink petals flutter to the ground. I caught one in my hand and felt its velvet softness, saw its tiny veins. Granmary had so loved natural beauty, especially flowers and trees. Maybe heaven was a garden, I thought, or maybe some exotic locale. How she had loved to travel!

I thought of her crocheting. She had still been working on the set of placemats for her nephew and his wife the last time I had seen her at her house. Was that what she had in her hand when she died? Had she ever finished them? The thought of them released the floodgates.

"Oh, Granmary," I sobbed out loud as I looked at the little pink petal in my hand. I cupped it hard.

I felt so guilty for crying instead of smiling that I only cried all the harder. My head was in my hands when I felt someone's hand on my shoulder.

"Mom, I—"

"It's not your mother," Matt said as I looked up. I smiled at him, but the smile didn't stick, and I could feel my chin quivering. He sat down beside me.

"You're missing her terribly, aren't you?" he asked. When I nodded, he added, "It's okay to cry."

"No, it's not," I told him. "She wanted me to celebrate her life, not to be sad."

"I'm sure she did, Beth, but sometimes before you get to the point of celebration, you have to be sad, you have to mourn. You can't just feel the void of loss and celebrate. Feel the loss, be sad that's she's gone, and then you're ready to move on to the point of celebrating her life."

A shower of cherry blossoms fell like snowflakes just then. It seemed like Granmary making a comment. She was telling me to listen to what Matt was saying.

"You're right," I told him, but when a breeze blew some of the blossoms off my arm and it seemed as though Granmary were again speaking, the moment seemed so profound that a new wave of tears washed into my eyes. "It's just . . . it's just . . . ."

"Here," Matt told me as he opened his arms. I went into them. He patted my back and held me closely, and once again, as I had when we were dancing, I smelled the scent of his soap, so fresh and clean, so . . . *Matt.*

"I'm better now," I finally told him, pulling away gently. I looked into his dark brown eyes and saw such concern that I knew I could talk to him about it. "I'd been holding back the tears. Matt, do you want to know what finally made the dam break?"

"Of course. Tell me."

"Well, she was making this set of placemats for her nephew and his wife. Thinking of her working so hard at it—she was always doing things for others, you know—and then not to quite get the set finished. Well, it just got to me, Matt. There are so many things everyone leaves behind."

He shifted his position on the bench a little so that he was facing me squarely.

"That's true, Beth, but Mrs. Sealy was eighty-nine. You told me she raised a family, was active in civic affairs, and traveled extensively, to name just a few things. She didn't give up or lose her special grace when she developed arthritis, eye problems, and heart trouble, either, and that's a lot more than many people are able to do. So yes, everyone leaves certain things unfinished, I suppose, and yet maybe we have to look at life another way. Look at what they got done instead of at what they didn't."

"Yeah, that makes sense. Actually, she told me she'd 'skipped through life most merrily.'"

"That's a wonderful way of putting it, isn't it? So, Beth, remember that's how she felt. Her nephew will treasure the mats she did get crocheted, just as you can treasure the teas you had with her and her friendship."

Yes!

"I will treasure them."

"Good," he answered. His face was such a wonderful picture of understanding that something turned over in my heart.

Follow your heart. Granmary's words again. It was time to tell Matt how I felt about something else.

"I never went with Brad to that basketball game," I told him.

"I know. I saw his buddy Jason pick him up that night. What made you change your mind?"

"I realized how stupid an idea it was. It wouldn't have been fair to Brad or true to myself to go. That poem you gave me was a deciding factor."

He nodded, looking pleased that the poem had helped.

"You know, I had forgotten about it for a long time. Then it turned up in my notebook with some diagrams of carrots, of all things, and some stanzas sort of jumped right out at me. If I were a poet, maybe I could have written it myself. I was hoping Brad would turn into someone else."

"You need someone who respects your convictions, listens to your ideas, and accepts you just as you are. And ultimately, Beth, you need someone you cherish."

"I cherish you," I told him quietly. It must have been too soft for him to hear. I was trying to decide whether or not to repeat it when I heard his voice.

"What did you say?" he asked.

"It was you I wanted Brad to be." I reached out my right hand and touched his cheek very lightly. As I pulled it back, I added, "Matt, I love you."

There. It was out in the open. Even as I realized I'd actually said it, I had these terrible mixed feelings. Would he turn and run and never speak to me again? Would he sweep me into his arms? Or worse than anything, would he laugh or not even care?

He had been sitting close to me on the stone bench. He started to get up but changed his mind and sat back down.

"Beth, that's a beautiful sentiment," he told me. His eyes looked directly into mine. I didn't see any amusement, any revulsion, anything negative. "You and I are great friends, and we have so much in common."

He took both of my hands and cupped his around them. They felt so warm and sheltering and right.

"Someone described love as 'friendship with wings.'"

"That's beautiful," I told him, feeling the warmth of his large hands radiating into mine.

"You've always been my little bird, haven't you?"

I nodded.

"Sometimes," he went on, "having things in common, getting along, and even loving isn't enough. Sometimes there are other considerations. You know I just turned twenty-three, and I know you are almost sixteen. At some other point in time, those seven years might be nothing, but right now, Beth . . . right now they matter.

"You talked a little while ago about all the things people never get done in a lifetime. I know you were talking about Granmary, but it can apply to us, too. You need to skip your own way along merrily, to discover all kinds of things in this big, wonderful world. I've discovered some of them just because I've lived a little longer, but I still have a great deal of 'skipping' of my own to do.

"We are free to love," he continued, "and yet there's more to it than that."

He rose and pulled me up with him. We were face-to-face.

My heart was bursting with emotion, and I tried to say something, but he placed a finger over my lips.

"Shh," he told me.

"Little Bird," he said as he placed his hands on my shoulders and held me at arms' length. The regret I saw in his eyes made my heart sink into my shoes. I wondered if he felt me trembling, or if I was trembling only in my mind and heart. "Little Bird, you must fly away."

"Matt."

"Shh," he told me again. Then he pulled me against his chest and held me closely. He kissed my hair and told me in the gentlest tone I'd ever heard, "Fly away, my Little Bird . . . for now."

And then something happened. As I felt his heart beating so strongly, I was amazed to realize that mine wasn't broken the way it might have been at one time. I'd come a long way lately, somehow, maybe through Granmary's death, through the trials of the divorce, through dealing with Kari, and yes, also because of Matt.

It was I who pulled away.

"I understand," I told him.

And I did.

The next few weeks flew by in sort of an unreal way as the trip loomed ever-nearer on my horizon. I was as excited as ever, but there was so much else going on that I had to steal time from other things to daydream and look through books on the places I was going to see.

Even though we were going during spring vacation, for one thing, I'd miss about a week of school, so I had to really study in preparation. Since the extra work forced my thoughts away from Granmary's death and from Kari's pranks, it was probably a good thing.

As for Matt, he continued to take me to school, and we still talked in the easy way we always had, about his student teaching, Egypt, Kari, and big and little issues. He didn't seem uncomfortable around me.

It didn't hurt to be around him, either. As the time to leave for Egypt approached, I carried Matt's message of the cherry blossoms tucked deeply within my heart.

Chapter Twelve

I'm really on my way to Egypt, I wrote in
my brand new travel journal. *We took off at
dawn and flew to John F. Kennedy International
Airport, where we boarded this plane. In
another three hours or so, we'll have a brief
stopover in Paris before the final leg of the
journey—to Cairo!*

*Everyone else in my row has been watching
the in-flight movie, but I have been reading in my
red* Baedeker's Egypt, *trying to memorize some
basic facts and to learn other, new things. I like
to know something about what I'm seeing when I
go on a trip. I think I'm finally getting some
dates straight:*

OLD KINGDOM: about 2640-2160 B.C.
MIDDLE KINGDOM: about 2040-1650 B.C.
NEW KINGDOM: about 1551-712 B.C.

*The guidebook explains that much is shrouded
in mystery. Dates vary some from source to
source, but no matter how you look at it, that's
so long ago! What is it going to be like to see
anything that ancient? There are also the more
recent Greek, Roman, and Islamic periods. So
much history! And I'm going to see it firsthand.*

*Whatever my feelings, it's going to be neat
to record all my reactions in this beautiful
journal,* I wrote as I ran my fingers over its

smooth leather cover.

Matt, I thought, remembering. He had handed me something wrapped in blue foil paper with a gold metallic ribbon. The leather of his gift inside was the same shade of blue as the wrapping paper, with gold lettering to match the ribbon.

"Read the inscription somewhere over the ocean," he said. As hard as waiting had been, I'd waited. Now it was time.

I caressed the leather again and then opened the front cover and felt my heart flip-flop as I saw his bold handwriting:

> Little Bird,
> Have an unforgettable trip as you
> make another dream come true.
>> Love,
>> Matt

"Love, Matt." Something soared inside me as I read those words. And he'd remembered our dancing. For just a moment, I saw us again, me in my white chiffon and Matt in his tux. I closed my eyes to savor the sensation. Then as I finally let the mental image go, I realized what a perfect gift the journal was. Each time I wrote in it, I would feel Matt with me.

I picked up my pen again and continued writing with:

> *Whatever else this trip turns out to be, it*
> *will definitely be a most unforgettable one.*

Hours later, I saw lots of activity around me. There was a run on the restrooms, flight attendants were busily picking up empty cups, and many passengers were looking expectantly out the windows.

The seatbelt sign went on and I felt our descent.

"What do you see?" I asked Kari, who had the window seat. Dad and Susan were two rows behind us.

"Nothing so far," she told me.

Then the plane tipped its right wing downward, and Kari excitedly shook my arm and pointed.

"Oh, my heavens!" I exclaimed, using a Granmary phrase. "Those are the Pyramids of Giza!"

Not taking her eyes off the astounding sight, Kari nodded.

For a few moments, we seemed poised forever above the famous landmarks, which looked almost like a mirage in the haze and desert dust.

Then I shivered in wonder as our plane touched that fabled ground and I knew they were real.

"We'll be right down the hall," Susan and Dad chorused much later as Dad put my bag onto a luggage rack.

"Don't worry about us," Kari said.

"We'll be fine," I assured them. Of course, "fine" was one of those words that people toss around very casually. We'd be fine if we didn't clobber each other first, I wanted to add.

"Remember to drink only bottled water," Susan reminded us. Then they were gone and we were alone.

Moments ticked by as we stood like statues in the room. Kari seemed as much at a loss for words as I felt. Well, I would at least try to break the ice.

"It's a nice room," I commented. Although it wasn't especially big or fancy, it had a lot of pretty wood closets, a sitting area with two chairs and a table, and a refrigerated mini-bar. Kari must also have been surveying the room.

"I'm glad it's not a double bed," she said.

"Me, too." As I looked at the twin beds, I thought that since Kari had had her choice of plane seats, it was only fair that I get to select my bed. I really needed the one closer to the bathroom anyway, since walking there without much light in the middle of the night could spell trouble with my balance. I assumed that Kari would want the bed by the window anyway. But just as I was starting to pat the one I wanted, she spoke up.

"I'll take this one," she said as she fell back onto it. It was the wrong one.

"Actually, I was going to volunteer to take that one," I told her, not really wanting to get into the balance thing. I didn't need her calling me names on our first day in Egypt. "This one by the window has a better view. I don't mind your taking it."

"Thanks, no," she told me huffily. I never knew what was going to ruffle Kari Quinn's feathers.

Should I let it go or stand up for my needs? I didn't want to make a big deal of it, but I didn't want to sprain an ankle in the middle of the night in a strange hotel room, either, just because I'd been a wimp.

Kari was sprawled on "my" bed with her hands under her head. I walked over close.

"Kari, there's sort of a special reason why I want the one you're on."

She sprang up into a sitting position.

"Yeah, and that's the reason, all right. You want it because it's the one I picked. Why don't you grow up, Beth Langford?"

I couldn't believe she was being so unreasonable.

"Take your precious bed then," I told her angrily. "If I stumble onto you during the night, don't blame *me*."

"Oh Beth, I see right through that one. Now you're using your handicap to get what you want. Well, it won't work. I don't feel like a pity party. I'm sticking with this one."

Total brat! I wondered how she would react

when I left the bathroom light on all night, with the bathroom door ajar to steer me there. I didn't bring that up just then. I'd had enough of her.

"Fine!" I said. "I'm going out onto the balcony."

"Fine!" rang out her answer.

I'd planned to go outside to stew, but stewing was totally impossible once I looked in front of me. Involuntarily, I shivered, hardly believing that the Pyramid of Cheops—the Great Pyramid—loomed mysteriously only a stone's throw away from me. The view had to be one of the most fantastic a hotel could have. It was, after all, one of the Seven Wonders of the Ancient World.

I felt my mind boggle as I thought how I was looking at something over four thousand years old. It wasn't quite close enough for me to pick out all the details, but I could see the huge honey-colored blocks that made up its shape. Time sort of fell away as in my mind's eye I saw the procession of the thousands who were said to have worked on its construction. For a moment, I smelled their sweat and felt their aching muscles as they built for all eternity.

I sat down on one of the balcony's chairs and recorded my impressions in the travel journal Matt had given me, adding a little about our wild ride to the hotel in Giza from the airport.

I didn't stumble and land on Kari's bed that night. I was so exhausted from the long flight and the excitement of being in Egypt that after a light dinner, I slept the night through.

Kari, of course, hogged the bathroom the next morning. She also let me know my curls looked frizzy. They might have looked better if I'd had a little more time in the bathroom, I wanted to say, but I just bit my lip.

After a buffet breakfast in the hotel's Greenery

115

restaurant, our Egyptian odyssey began as we rode by cab from Giza to Cairo proper, where our destination was the Egyptian Museum. "I like to start with museums when I travel," Granmary had said, "for an overview."

Just getting there was an adventure. Greater Cairo was a city of millions, with people milling everywhere, for one thing. That included on roadways that didn't even have lines down them to mark any lanes. Traffic moved in snaking lines, and what in America would have been three orderly lanes somehow became four, or even five, in Cairo. I'd never seen streets so haphazardly crammed.

I watched in horror as a woman walked out into the stream of traffic, but she made it across in sort of a strange, darting dance. I wondered why she hadn't gone to the next crosswalk or stoplight, until I realized there didn't seem to be any. Only a few of the biggest intersections even had signals.

The street sounds were almost deafening, so it's no wonder that when Dad turned around to say something, I didn't hear him over countless blaring horns, people's voices, and the rise and fall of something I couldn't identify. It sounded like somebody moaning. But Dad pointed to my left and mouthed, "Look!"

"A donkey!" I exclaimed in wonder. I mean, this was a busy city, and a donkey pulling an old wooden cart on a street with so many cars seemed so otherworldly: a *juxtaposition*, I thought, remembering a word I'd picked up somewhere. Inside the cart was a heap of something white and green—vegetables of some kind, I guessed. "What's inside the cart?" I shouted to Dad over the noise.

He shrugged his shoulders and then spoke to our cab driver. A moment later, Dad said something else to me. I didn't get it, though, so he told Kari.

Looking irritated that she had to be the go-between, she finally said into my hearing aid, "Garlic."

At some point, it became obvious that our cabbie was taking us to the museum by a roundabout route. Maybe it was a shortcut. Anyway, we got into a section of the city where there were fewer people and little traffic. The people here didn't dress like most of the Egyptians I had seen so far. Our cab driver had on slacks and a plaid shirt, and most of the hotel people wore regular western-style clothing.

Now, though, there were no pants and shirts combinations or street-length dresses. Then men were in traditional *galabias*, the long, flowing nightshirt-type garments that desert people had worn for centuries. The women and little girls wore long dresses and scarves to cover their heads. I thought how hot they must be in the summer months, but I knew that covering up was part of their religion.

The people looked content as they went about their daily business. Still, the poverty of the scene broke my heart. Did people still live this way?

No one seemed to be starving, but women were washing their families' clothes in a dirty-looking little stream where garbage actually floated. I noticed a woman filling a jug with the water. They didn't drink that, did they, or cook with it?

We passed an open-air market along the same stream, where slabs of meat were hanging on hooks in the warm air. There were also fish with their heads still on. Their dead eyes stared out at us as flies buzzed around. In a moment of shared feeling, Kari and I looked at each other and said, "Eww!"

A slight breeze blew dust onto the people, meat, and fish, but no one seemed to care.

We could also see a big change in the buildings, which were multi-family and made of poor quality bricks and mortar. They weren't old, but already they looked like they were falling apart. In fact, although people obviously lived in many of the apartments, other, empty units were exposed with a wall missing, sort of like the back of a dollhouse.

Then gradually the scene changed back. There were nicer buildings, more cars, and the people looked like business people, shoppers, and a mix of big-city street life. The main difference from other cities was the occasional donkey or *galabia*.

The big brown museum was in a good area not too far from the Nile.

I loved museums, and this one was a perfect walk through the thousands of years of Egyptian history. We saw everything from mummies to papyrus with hiero-glyphics to colossal statues of pharaohs and gods. There were tiny amulets, modest household items, and the blazing treasures of boy-king "Tut."

Susan and Dad had seen the King Tut exhibit in Seattle many years before, so they walked through fairly quickly. Kari and I took our time.

"This is really something," she commented as we made our way around case after case of gleaming gold. Even though it was so old, each piece was so well-crafted—such a perfect work of art—that it gave me a new respect for the Ancients.

"It's stupendous," I agreed. "And it will be really neat to see his actual tomb in the Valley of the Kings soon," I added with a little anticipatory shiver.

"Yeah," Kari said.

I was walking around the beautiful, burnished gold mask inlaid with gemstones when I felt my ankle hit something hard. At the same time I realized it was a guardrail protecting one of the most cherished of all Egyptian finds, I started to lose my balance. *Oh no! Don't let me fall. Not here,* I prayed as the horrible image of crashing into the glass case went through my mind. Then somehow I managed to right myself. My relief soon turned to irritation, though.

"Clumsy," Kari made a point of saying all too clearly into my good ear. And there was that awful snicker of hers.

"It's not funny," I told her. "I could have fallen into that glass." Did she have an ounce of empathy?

"Well, you didn't, did you?"

That wasn't the point, but I let it pass. Still, a brief timeout from her before we met Susan and Dad in another part of the museum would be refreshing.

"Do you know which way the restroom is?" I asked her. Since she and Susan had gone when we'd first entered the museum, I knew she did. Dad and I had gone on ahead and I hadn't paid much attention.

"Yeah," she told me as we walked down a corridor, "See that door over there? Go through it and you'll almost be there."

But it was Kari up to her old tricks again. The door creaked open and led into some kind of storeroom filled with dusty statues and other museum odds and ends. If I hadn't been so tired of Kari's pranks, I might have been fascinated by the slightly sinister aura of the closed-off room, but as it was, I knew I wasn't supposed to be there and just left. Would she never stop?

Kari sort of put on a different face when my dad was around, so lunch went fine, and I even liked the Egyptian flat bread and spicy *tahina* sauce on my meatballs.

That afternoon, we continued our tour of Cairo with a trip to the 12th Century Citadel of Cairo, which rose high above us as our cab neared its massive outline. As I saw its huge walls and squat towers, I wondered whether or not they'd been made from stones used from some of the smaller pyramids. Granmary had said something about that. Whatever, it had *fortress* written all over it. There were even crenellations and slits in the towers for archers.

Yet it was different than most. Offsetting its medieval bulk were the tall, slender minarets of Mohammed Ali Mosque—the Alabaster Mosque—which sat on top of the whole thing.

"Look around Cairo," Granmary had said, "and you'll see layer upon layer of civilizations." The Islamic influence was just one of the many.

The way up was long and steep, and since I had to use my step-by-step incline approach, my mind was sort of blank of anything else as we made our way up. Matt would have held me firmly, I thought at one point. If I hadn't been so engrossed on getting up there, I might have resented the way Dad and Susan had gone on ahead, while Kari skipped along with the normal kind of balance I envied. I made it, though.

We all met briefly at the top of the Citadel.

"Now don't get separated," Dad warned as he looked from me to Kari. We settled on an easy-to-find meeting spot. "We'll meet you at four o'clock," he added. Then he and Susan were off in their own direction. They looked like the newlyweds they were.

"Let's—" Kari and I looked at each other and gave an uneasy laugh. We'd both started talking at once.

"You first," I invited.

"No, you," she said.

We were both trying, but we were at an impasse even when we tried to be polite.

"Okay," I finally said. "I was going to say, let's look at the view before going into the mosque."

"Sounds fine with me." From the way she said it, I think she had been about to say the same thing. She hurried on up ahead, and I followed at my slower pace. When I got there, I wasn't disappointed in the spot she'd chosen.

From up high, as far as my eyes could see, Cairo spread before me in a grayish expanse. Domes and the pencil-slim minarets of lots of mosques dotted the view in the warm afternoon. Shimmering in the hazy heat, the Pyramids of Giza sat perched, timeless and tranquil, on the horizon.

"They look like a mirage," I said, pointing to the famous triangular shapes in the distance.

"They really do," Kari agreed. She moved to my other side then, and I didn't get all she said: " . . . different . . . ."

"What?" I asked. Up high like this, a little bit away from the traffic noises of the busy city, it was quieter, but Kari had talked into my bad ear. I was sort of surprised when she picked up on it and switched sides.

"Sorry. You're right. They look like they might disappear any minute. I said before that they look so different each time we see them."

"Yeah," I agreed. It felt really weird to actually agree with her on anything.

"Are you ready to go inside the mosque?" she asked sort of impatiently. I was eager to see it, too, but the view really grabbed me. Each time I looked, I saw more minarets and the view seemed even more delectably foreign. I put my hands on the wall at the edge of the giant stone outcropping and craned my neck.

"Not quite. This view is just so terrific. I can't believe we're really here."

I looked out for awhile more and then became aware of Kari's silence. I assumed that she was also savoring the scene, but when I finally looked at her, her eyes were fastened on my scarab ring.

Should I let it go and just walk into the mosque, or should we finally have it out, here and now, about Granmary's gift to me? I really did want to make peace, especially during this trip, but what was the right way to go about it?

"Are you still mad about the ring?" I finally asked.

"'The ring'?"

"I saw you looking at it," I told her, wiggling my finger.

"Oh. No, I like mine," she said, looking down at her signet pinkie ring.

"It's very pretty," I told her. It was gleaming a rich gold in the afternoon sun.

Let it go or say more? Let it go or say more? I kept debating.

"Let's go inside," she said. She started to turn away, and that made my decision for me.

I reached for her arm. She pulled away even though I'd barely touched it, but she stopped.

"Kari, maybe we should talk about it. I mean, you wonder why Granmary gave this to me, don't you?"

"If you want to put it that way, sort of. I know you went to her house a lot after Mom married your dad. Why?"

"Yeah. I did. I liked Granmary a lot, Kari."

"Well, you think I didn't?"

"Of course not."

"*Granmary.* You had to even call her that, didn't you?"

"I didn't at first."

"Yeah, but you moved right in."

Maybe now wasn't the time to talk about this. I could see how jealous Kari was. I knew there must be more to it, but I couldn't quite figure it out. *You're such a baby, Kari Quinn,* I thought. Well, I didn't want to fight.

"Let's go inside," I said. This time it was she who just stood there. I was glad. I couldn't let her think I'd "moved right in" on her great-grandmother. "We'll talk about this later," I said. Then more softly, I added, "She always asked about you, Kari."

Kari digested that last part and let the rest go.

"Okay, let's," she agreed. Somehow, I knew the Granmary subject was going to come up again.

We walked into the Alabaster Mosque's tiled forecourt.

"Wow," Kari said. "Look at those porch things and that fountain. Isn't that where the Muslims wash their feet before going in to worship?"

"It must be." I was just as amazed by the "porch things," as Kari had called them. I'd seen in the guide-book that they were vaulted galleries.

An attendant stopped us and tied paper booties over our shoes, and then we forgot our differences as we walked into the building.

"It's so big," Kari commented softly.

"And beautiful," I whispered. The huge prayer hall's big open floor space was covered with unmatched Oriental carpets where pews would be in a church. There were tapestries on the walls, and dozens of glass globes hung from the ceiling to give the mosque a candlelike glow.

The *minbar*, or pulpit, was elaborately decorated. The iman wasn't there, but I remembered Granmary's description of the way it went. His assistants stood on the *dikka*, a platform supported on columns, so that the congregation could see and imitate stuff like his genuflections.

As my eyes traveled around the prayer hall, they finally looked upward.

"Look," I whispered to Kari as I pointed to the inside of the great Byzantine dome. She drew in her breath as her hand went over her chest, and I wondered if she saw it the same way I did.

The dome's intricately patterned interior blazed

with gilt, and the small stained glass windows that circled it looked exactly like jewels set into the hemisphere. Rubies, sapphires, and topazes shone richly.

"Wow!" Kari mouthed.

Since we both knew about the "wishing arches" from Granmary, we walked over to an arched green-and-gold wooden structure to the side of the prayer hall and made wishes.

On the way out, we peeked into a side room and saw the tomb of Mohammed Ali.

"That was really something," I said as we finally walked back outside.

"Yeah. It's funny. Most people only think of the pharaohs and stuff when they think of Egypt. They forget about the more recent history. Not that this place is new," she laughed.

"Hardly," I agreed, since I remembered that the Citadel of Cairo was begun in 1176 A.D. by Saladin. What a different time that had been. I remembered reading in the guidebook that just to get water up to the top, oxen on a platform part of the way down a shaft had turned a wheel. Joseph's Well, it had been called. Maybe that square thing I was seeing was the shaft. When I pointed it out to Kari, she thought it was neat.

How could we get along so well talking about stuff like this? I wondered as we explored more of the Citadel. She wasn't even calling me Boozy Beth as I stumbled over the uneven courtyards and pathways.

By the time we met Dad and Susan, we were tired, and so were they. We settled on dinner at the hotel.

Afterwards, as they left us at our room, Dad said, "I thought tomorrow we'd all ride camels by the Pyramids."

"Fun!" said Kari.

And my heart sank.

Chapter Thirteen

Kari drifted off to sleep, as far as I could tell, but I must have lain awake half the night.

Did Dad really expect me to ride a camel? I tried to picture myself on top of one of the swaying, dipping "ships of the desert" and knew in my heart that it would be stupid to try it. If I didn't fall off from the lurching, I'd at least wreck my balance even further, maybe to the point of making me throw up, and I didn't want to spoil my time in Egypt.

The thoughts buzzed in my mind like an angry bee. Then sometime in the night I finally fell asleep.

"Kari," I said the next morning after she came out of the bathroom. She had on one of the many-pocketed khaki pants and a shrimp-colored camp shirt. Dressed and ready to go, I thought. "When you go down to the breakfast room, would you mind asking Dad to come in here for a minute? I want to talk to him alone about something."

She gave me a weird look, but agreed, and after tying her hair back into a ponytail, she went to find him.

A camel? I just didn't understand Dad sometimes. He'd known me all my life. Hadn't he noticed that certain things, like my balance, had changed after I was sick? Why did I get the feeling that he was trying to make me into somebody I wasn't?

Even worse, was Kari Quinn everything he wanted me to be?

I caught my reflection in the mirror over the dresser as I walked out onto the balcony. I, too, wore khakis and a camp shirt. I looked as ready to go as Kari did. But in my case, I thought as I walked on, looks were deceiving.

I gazed at the view and tried to empty my thoughts of mundane things. Again, I was struck by the timelessness of the scene. It sounds crazy, but right then I sort of envied the Great Pyramid. I mean, it was just there, free of human problems, unless you wanted to count pollution and people hacking away sometimes at its stones. No, maybe it wasn't so good even to be an age-old wonder of the world. I didn't know. I just knew I was tired of the way things were.

"Beth?" I jumped slightly as Dad's voice cut into my thoughts. I hadn't seen or heard him walk onto the balcony. "Susan and Kari are waiting in the Greenery." Then he looked at the Pyramid and said, "It's a stagger-ing sight, isn't it?"

"Yeah." Now wasn't the time to talk about that, though. "Dad, I'm not going on the camel ride. I just wanted to let you know that in private. I just can't do it."

A look I'd seen all too often crossed his face, and I felt sort of sick.

"Don't be a spoilsport, Beth. How do you know you can't if you won't even try?"

In a way, he had a point. In fact, a motto of mine ever since I was about twelve had been that it was better to try and fail than never to try at all. And I had done things, like dancing to the Viennese waltz with Matt, that I never believed I'd really be doing, but there was a difference. Matt had tailored that dance to my needs. I also didn't have a trip at stake then. Oh, no, I believed in trying. But I also lived with myself day in and day out. I knew what was foolhardy.

Dad was still staring at me with that look. Why did I have to do any explaining at this point in my life? Why did I have to let him down by just being me? I thought of Matt again, remembering that wonderful feeling of being happy I was Beth, not Ginger Rogers or anyone else. With Matt I just sort of was. Why couldn't he accept me that way? Could I somehow get Dad to understand that I had to be me?

"It's like tennis, Dad," I tried to explain. "My balance."

"Oh, come on," he scoffed. "It's not the same at all. You just have to sit there and let the animal do the work."

Oh, boy . . . .

"I'm not going, Dad," I said again. I needed something he could relate to. I thought a minute and went on with, "Remember the time I tried horseback riding?"

He didn't say yes or no, but I could tell by his expression that he did. My equilibrium trouble had been so set off then that it had gone on for days. For the longest time, Dad just stood there looking at the view. Then finally, he spoke.

"All right, then. But come along, and you can find some shade while we have fun. Let's go down and have some breakfast."

"Okay," I told him. I felt such a strange mixture of relief, hurt, and anger that I needed a little time to pull myself together. "I'll be there in a minute. You go ahead."

"Don't be too long," he said as he turned to leave.

"I won't," I promised.

Even though he wasn't forcing me to ride on the camel, he just didn't get the picture. Worse, he had had to rub it in. Did he really have to add that part about my finding some shade while they had their fun?

I continued to mull things over in my mind as I stepped outdoors on the way to the breakfast room. I was so deep in thought, in fact, that I all but walked into a hotel employee I'd seen in the lobby a couple of times.

"Excuse me," I told the man. "I wasn't paying

attention." About thirty, I guessed, he had beautiful tea-colored skin, but even though he was dressed in western-style clothing, I doubted that the Egyptian spoke English. My apology had been automatic.

"That's quite all right. You were thinking about your day's adventures?" he asked in such perfect British English that I was amazed. He flashed me a blinding smile that showed his even teeth. I realized that I had stopped dead in my tracks and must be staring at him.

"Your perfect English startled me," I explained. I saw that his nametag read Asmie.

"I went to school in England," he told me.

"That explains it," I said with a nod. "You were right. I was thinking about the day. We're going over closer to the Pyramids."

"How do you like my country?"

"It's just wonderful but I haven't seen much of it yet."

"I hope your journey takes you to Upper Egypt," he said, referring to the area where Karnak and the famous tombs were.

"Oh yes, I'm really looking forward to that," I told him enthusiastically. "We're going there in a few days."

"Good. Enjoy your stay, Miss . . . ."

"Langford. Beth Langford."

"And I am Asmie," he informed me with another smile as he began walking on his way. So did I.

The brief encounter with the friendly man had somehow made me feel calmer. My breakfast didn't taste quite as much like cardboard as I thought it would.

There were about a half-dozen camels standing around, wearing tasseled halters in different bright colors. Camel tenders in flowing robes stood nearby smoking cigarettes as they waited for the next round of tourist riders. I heard the strange cadence of Arabic. The strong camel smell, which might have been a stench anywhere else in the world, somehow fit the scene perfectly.

"Is it me," Susan asked, "or do those camels seem to be smiling?"

Dad and Kari gave her a weird sideways look, but when I looked at the nearest dromedary, his mouth just did naturally curve upward, and I saw what Susan meant.

"They do look like it," I agreed. "Let me take your picture before they lead you away."

I snapped a couple of Susan and Kari after they were on top of the tall animals, and although I was happy for them, it also hurt to see their anticipation and know I wasn't going. I could almost taste the adventure. Should I try it anyway? But then I thought of Matt: ". . . recognizing and accepting one's limitations is paradoxically a strength." No, I'd stick to my guns.

Dad made one more stab at trying to get me to go.

"Won't you even try?" he asked. My heart sank. I could tell he thought I was a total wimp.

"I have to listen to my instincts here, Dad. Please understand. Susan and Kari are waiting. Please just go."

The camel tender was waiting for him. Even the ruby-tasseled beast snorted in impatience.

"All right, then," Dad finally agreed. He shook his head and added, "Your mother's done this to you. It's not your fault."

Then he was climbing into the saddle of the kneeling camel. I took his picture. The man in the *galabia* led them away, and as Dad looked back at me to wave, I waved back.

He never saw my tears.

I found a little dot of shade and swigged bottled

water as I watched their shapes disappear behind a long, low building.

Spoilsport! I'd danced with Matt. I'd ridden in a hot air balloon even though my stomach had been tied into knots at first. And I'd tried things, like the horseback riding, that had stirred up the nausea and vomiting. No, I wasn't a spoilsport. I'd just learned the hard way when to try new things and when not to.

Plain of Giza
Camel Staging Area

I vowed not to write lots of personal stuff in this journal, which is supposed to be a travel journal, not a personal diary, but let's just say I'm finding that just because you go thousands of miles   from home doesn't mean you automatically leave all your troubles there. Dad is still Dad. Kari is still Kari. And I . . . well . . . of course I'm still me.

And yet maybe I'm not quite the same. Being here makes me think of things I don't normally think about. For one thing, I think of the age of the Pyramids and the Great Sphinx and I feel sort of insignificant in the whole scheme of things. I mean, just think how many people have lived and died since these monuments went up. It's mind-boggling. What did my English teacher call this? Oh yes, the transience of human existence. I can't help but feel that now. Humans are on earth such a short time compared to something like a pyramid. I felt it some when Granmary died, but it's an even more profound feeling in the shadow of these ancient monuments. She was just one person, and her time on earth

....
130

*overlapped mine. But the people who built these
and who have come and gone—they lived and
breathed so very long ago. Will another person
my age sit here writing in her travel journal
hundreds of years from now, when I am only
dust?*

I felt really alive, though, when we walked
through the merchandise-crammed alleys of a big open-
air bazaar later that day. Even though I got jostled a lot,
I was struck by the delectable foreignness of vendors
ranting in Arabic; the smell of exotic spices, searing
lamb, and incense; the sight of shoppers with baskets on
their heads near stalls of carpets, a welter of baubles,
and clothing highlighted full-length against canvas
"walls"; and the feel of new fabrics, inlaid boxes, and
rough baskets.

Kari poked me in the ribs when she spotted some
belly dancing costumes.

"Aren't they cool?" she asked.

"Cool," I agreed. And gaudy. Their neon-bright
colors almost called for sunglasses.

"You buy?" a vendor with yellowed teeth asked
as I fingered a lime green outfit with oodles of sequins
on it. Kari's eyes were on a hot pink one. They would
make great costumes for parties even if we never got
around to learning how to belly dance.

"We buy . . . maybe," I told him.

"Yeah," Kari put in. "How much?"

The vendor named a price in Egyptian pounds
and then sucked in deeply on his cigarette. As best as
we could, we calculated the pounds into dollars. It didn't
really come to that much, but we knew we were
supposed to bargain, so we named a price about half of
the vendor's. When he shook his head vehemently and
spouted something in rapid Arabic, we guessed we'd

gone too low. We finally settled on a price about two-thirds of his original offer.

"Will Dad and your mom kill us if we get them?" I asked. They were several stalls up ahead, by a spice vendor.

Kari shrugged and said, "They aren't any worse than a ballet costume."

"Yeah, and they wouldn't have given us money to spend in the bazaar if they hadn't meant us to," I added.

"Let's do it!" we said almost in unison.

"We'll take these," I told the man, and as he wrapped them in cheap paper, Kari and I looked at each other and giggled.

When I looked around this time, I didn't see Dad and Susan, and suddenly there was something sinister about the very foreign, exotic bazaar, with all its strange sights, sounds, and scents. It was like having fallen into a James Bond thriller. Anything could happen. Kari must also have felt the aura of potential intrigue.

"There's a spooky feeling here," she commented with a little shiver.

I nodded as we stuck close together. It was a relief when we finally spotted Dad and Susan again.

Kari seemed to be in an unusually good mood that evening in our room. We admired our belly dancing costumes again.

"I thought they'd freak out," I said. Instead, Dad and Susan had only rolled their eyes good-naturedly.

"Me too, but when I saw that Lawrence of Arabia robe Mom bought for your dad, I understood it better. I bet he bought her something too. Oh wow, you don't think—" When she broke out laughing, it was infectious.

Through my laughter, I said, "A belly dancing costume? Yeah, I'll bet there was one in that package."

This time we rolled our eyes.

"Well, since we can't wow anyone with ours now, want to watch a little TV and order some Oriental sweets?"

"That sounds great to me," I told her. I didn't want to start thinking about the camel thing again and could use some escape.

An hour later, we were finishing the sweet little pastries and were caught up in a French drama that was dubbed in Arabic. Even with the language problem, we could figure out that Monique was married to Jean-Paul, who was old enough to be her grandfather, but that her true love was handsome but poor Luc. Jean-Paul had found out that Monique was seeing Luc, so she was treading a fine line between trying to keep her husband and continuing to see Luc.

Some haunting music came on as the picture faded out.

"Oh, no, it's a serial," I said. Kari got up and turned the small television set off.

"We'll never find out if Jean-Paul and Luc square off," she said.

"Or if Monique can stay in those fabulous designer gowns," I laughed.

"Yeah." Kari laughed too as she made her way over to the tray from room service. "Want to split this last Oriental sweet?"

"Okay. Did you ever wonder why they call them Oriental sweets?"

"Yeah. With all the honey and nuts, they're pretty much like baklava. Isn't that Greek? I never thought of Greece being the Orient, did you?"

"Nope. Maybe at one time Greece seemed pretty far east."

"Right." She yawned then and added, "I'm pretty pooped all of a sudden."

"Me too," I said. Her yawn had been infectious. I hadn't gotten all that much sleep the night before. I brushed my teeth while she slipped into her pajamas, and then it was her turn in the bathroom.

As she came out, I said, "Would you mind going back in and turning the light on?" She knew the night-light routine but had forgotten. I saw her eyes roll, but she didn't make any comment as she did what I'd asked.

I waited until the bedroom lamps were off before I took off my hearing aid and carefully set it onto the bedside table. I liked to keep it on until the last minute, sort of like people who wear glasses wait to take them off and then keep them handy.

If I thought about camels, I don't remember. I must have fallen asleep as soon as my head hit the pillow.

I had to go to the bathroom in the middle of the night, though, and woke up. The first thing I realized was that the bathroom light was off. The hotel room was really dark, with just a few big, dim shapes. I lay there for a minute or two, trying to talk myself out of the need to go, but it didn't work.

Should I turn on the bedside lamp? That would have given me instant light, but I didn't really want to wake Kari up. Things had been a little better before we'd fallen asleep. Why rock the boat by blasting her awake in the middle of the night?

Gingerly, I slid out of bed, backing around so that I could use my hands to feel my way along its length. At the end, I slowly stood all the way up and tried to get my bearings. I could see the outline of Kari's bed in the dimness, but the bathroom itself was swallowed in blackness down near the doorway that led into the hotel's central hall.

Feel with your feet and hands. Take a step. Look around. Stop.

....

Whoever would have thought just getting to the bathroom could be so much work? I was doing okay by feeling my way along the closet wall, but I had to let go and walk across the room to get to where I thought the bathroom was. As I remembered, the space between the walls at that point wasn't more than a few feet. I ought to be able to make it.

Feel with your—

Then I was falling! Just as I let go of the wall, my right foot had touched something. Kari's shoe? Who would think a little thing like a shoe could throw off my balance? I reeled in the dark and landed right across the foot of Kari's bed.

Please don't let her wake up, I thought.

But the room was suddenly flooded with light, and I saw Kari sitting bolt upright in bed. She said something. I couldn't hear her words at all because my hearing aid was on the other side of the room.

"I'm sorry, Kari," I told her. "I was on my way to the bathroom, but the light was off and I lost my balance."

"Blah, blah, blah . . . ." There was nothing I could distinguish.

"Let me go to the bathroom," I said. If she made any comment to that, I didn't know. At least my bladder hadn't burst all over her bed, I thought, laughing to myself at the image.

I thought maybe she would be playing 'possum when I returned, but she was still sitting up straight, obviously waiting for some kind of explanation.

"Blah, blah, blah . . . ."

"Just a sec, Kari. I don't have my hearing aid on," I said as I walked past her. I felt her stare with each step. When I reached my hearing aid, I brushed my hair back and eased the aid into my ear. Kari watched in fascination.

" . . . doing," she was shouting as the sound came

back in.

"What did you say?"

"I was yelling at you and you didn't even hear."

"Well, that's the idea of a hearing aid."

"You're deaf without it?"

"Not quite. I hear some sounds, but words don't come in right."

"Oh," she said. "What was going on, anyway? I was fast asleep and felt this thud on my bed. I thought it was a burglar."

To anybody else, I would have apologized again, but I was mad that she'd turned the light off in the first place.

"It was just me," I told her. "Did you leave the light off in the bathroom?"

"So what if I did?"

"Well, I was trying to get there in the dark, and I tripped."

I expected her to comment on my tripping. Would she call me Boozy Beth right then and there? But when she spoke again, the subject was entirely different.

"How come you didn't go on the camel today?" she asked.

A longing to have been on the beast vibrated through me again—along with a streak of envy because she had gone and I hadn't been able to. I didn't want to start thinking again of Dad's pushiness.

"Oh, it seemed sort of hot," I told her. Lame excuse, Beth, I thought.

"Well, it wasn't bad, and the ride was lots of fun. I can't wait to show everybody the pictures."

"I think I got some good ones of you," I said.

I was just going to ask her if she wanted to try to get some more sleep when she spoke again.

"Are you jealous of me?" she asked.

"Jealous?" The question took me totally off-guard.

"Yeah."

"Me? Well, I wish I could walk as easily as you do and do stuff like play tennis."

"That's not what I meant. Or maybe it is, sort of. You mentioned the tennis thing. I mean, are you jealous of the things I do with your dad?"

"I could ask you the same thing about your mom. Are you jealous of me?"

"You're answering a question with a question. I'm talking about you, Beth."

"Okay, sure, I'd like to be able to play tennis with him the way you do."

"And go to Moeller's?"

"That too," I admitted. It was really the ice cream thing that bothered me. I mean, I'd had balance trouble for so long that it was almost a way of life for me, but Moeller's? That had been Dad's and my place.

"Yeah, but do you know what your dad talks about over those shakes?" she asked.

"Your brilliant lobs, I'm sure."

"Well, don't be so sure."

"What do you mean?" I asked.

"You. He talks about you and your accomplishments."

"Dad?" Were we talking about the same Bruce Langford?

"Yeah. Think about it for a while."

And I did.

Chapter Fourteen

Early the next morning, before anyone else was up, I took a walk around the hotel grounds, past eucalyptus trees, the poolside cafe, and the old section of the hotel, which was pretty in an almost lacy kind of way. Islamic Arabesque, Susan had called the architecture. As a real estate agent, she knew her building styles.

The Egyptian with the British English—Asmie, I remembered—waved at me. His greeting was drowned out by the noise of the hose he used to wash off the sidewalk. He looked busy, so I didn't stop, but I waved back.

The Great Pyramid played hide-and-seek with me as I walked. Sort of like our Mt. Hood at home, it looked different at different times of the day. Today, when I did see it, it didn't even look quite three-dimensional in the faint morning light. I was glad I'd put on a sweater. Without the early-spring sun warming me yet, I felt chilly.

Good. Maybe the cool air would clear my head.

The middle-of-the-night conversation with Kari played over in my mind. What had she said? That Dad sometimes talked about me and my accomplishments? What did he even know about my life anymore anyway? I mean, he was so wrapped up in his new family. It wasn't that I begrudged the time he spent with them, but when was the last time just he and I had done anything together? True, I couldn't play tennis with him like Kari did, but when was the last time he'd taken just me to a movie or to Moeller's for ice cream? We'd even used to go fishing together—just Dad and me without Mom—and we'd talk hour after hour about all kinds of things.

He knew my "accomplishments" then because he asked and he was there to see them firsthand, but when had he asked lately about what was really going on in my life?

The sound of something startled me. It was that moaning again. The *muezzin*, I'd learned, calling the faithful to prayer. The sound of his voice wafted over all the city, but usually I couldn't hear it clearly because it got mixed in with all the other city noises. But here, right now, it was quiet, and I listened to the strange rise and fall that sounded so much like a moan.

When I looked back toward the hotel, Asmie had stopped hosing the sidewalk and was down low on his knees facing Mecca in prayer. I looked away. I didn't know if watching was bad manners.

I looked for the Pyramid of Cheops, but I couldn't see it from where I was. Some trees and a hill blocked my view. The sun was getting stronger, and I was curious to see how it looked in the increasing light, so I braved the driveway, which sloped downward at that point. I was doing okay in one of my step-by-step approaches, but a horrible noise suddenly blasted into my ear.

Honk, honk!

Bus, my brain translated.

I saved myself from the big tour bus by sidestepping, but of course I wrecked my step-by-step incline approach by moving so quickly. I fell hard. The bus plowed on past me. As I started to get up, I felt my hand smarting, and when I looked at it, it was bleeding.

"Are you all right?" I heard a very British voice asking. Asmie. He helped me up.

"Thank you," I told him. "Yes, I'm fine. That bus just seemed to come out of nowhere."

"I saw it. He was not actually that close and would not have hit you. I will have a word with the driver, however. He was going too fast."

"Oh, that's all right. He just startled me. My balance is bad on slopes," I explained, "and anyone else probably wouldn't even have fallen. I just moved too fast. But thanks."

"I will help you to your room," he offered.

"Oh, that's very nice of you, but I just scraped my hand a little. It's really not necessary."

He must have realized that I was all right. We smiled, and then I was back on my way to the room.

I couldn't believe my eyes when I opened the door.

"What are you doing?" I asked.

Kari jumped at the sound of my voice. I walked closer to her.

"You're reading my travel journal! You never stop, do you?"

Still holding it, she said, "I wasn't reading it. I saw it there on the desk and just picked it up. It has a beautiful binding."

Could I believe her? It wasn't that there was anything that personal in my writings, but it was the principle. A diary was a private thing. And then there was Matt's inscription. What would Kari make of that?

She must have noticed then that I was a bit worse for the wear from my fall.

"Is that blood on your hand?" she asked as she set the book down. I let the journal thing pass. She could be telling the truth. But then again, it would be like Kari to snoop.

"Yeah," I told her. "I almost got creamed by a bus out on the driveway. I'm going to put a little antiseptic on it and it'll be fine." I turned toward the bathroom, and as I caught my reflection in the mirror, I also realized that my jeans were dirty from the fall. I'd have to change.

" . . . stupid . . . ."

....
140

I didn't wait around to hear what Kari was saying.

She played tennis all morning with Dad while Susan and I browsed among the shops in the main part of the hotel. We bought some inlaid mother-of-pearl boxes as gifts and had tea in the poolside cafe, which had come to life since my early morning walk. Susan and I talked about Granmary, books we liked, and so forth, and about that afternoon's destination of Memphis and Saqqara.

Dad rented a car for the trip, which I thought would take us straight out into the desert. Instead, we traveled through lush Nile-irrigated countryside on a two-lane road that followed an ancient canal. The scenery was like something out of another time.

In green fields broken by stands of tall date palms, men in *galabias* tended rows of corn, but instead of using tractors or even animal-driven plows, they bent down and used crude hand tools. There were donkeys everywhere—in the fields and on the road with riders on their backs or pulling carts piled high with crops. They all looked alike with their mottled gray-and-white coats and the same gentle but bored look on their faces. The houses along the route were low buildings made of mud brick, palm, and other natural materials. Now and then we spotted people in black, head-to-toe attire: Bedouins.

"Look!" I suddenly said in wonder, pointing to the left by the canal.

"A water wheel," Susan said in surprise as she turned around momentarily and clapped her hands in delight. Then her gaze went from us back to the strange sight. The water wheel, or *saqiya,* was a waist-high horizontal wheel about eight feet in diameter. This one was powered by an ox as a little girl who looked around nine years old supervised.

With her bare feet, a dress that was timeless in its

faded shapelessness, and a length of bright cloth over her head that trailed down her back Madonna-style, she might have leapt straight from a Bible story.

"She looks like someone in a Sunday school pamphlet picture," Kari remarked. I nodded. It was amazing how sometimes she had the same reaction I did.

Then we were passing bright green alfalfa fields.

I knew we were close to Memphis when we turned off the road and passed through a quiet little village. People still lived there, but the great ancient city of Memphis, which had been very important in its day, was long gone. We could see a few scattered stones and broken columns of the old city at the sides of the road as we made our way to a tourist stop.

"Not much left," Dad commented as he parked the car in a small lot.

"Remember what Granmary said, Bruce: 'Sometimes less is more,'" Susan reminded.

"Right," Dad said with affection. He'd also loved Susan's grandmother. "And at least it's not overrun with tourists." Dad was right, I saw as I looked around. Here there were only two or three other cars and one bus, compared to the hordes of tour buses and people at places like the Egyptian Museum.

"We'll have our picnic after we look around a little," Susan said, leaving the hamper the hotel people had fixed for us in the car.

Our first stop was an open-air building especially constructed to house the colossal statue of Rameses II, the 19th Dynasty pharaoh who had reigned for sixty-seven years. He was a really important one, I knew, who had built a lot of temples.

"Didn't Granmary say that about half the existing temples in Egypt date back to Rameses II's time in the thirteenth century B.C.?" I asked no one in particular as

....
142

we walked along.

Dad shrugged, and Kari didn't seem to know, but Susan said she thought that sounded right.

"Oh, there he is," she said with a certain wonder in her voice.

When I moved up, I could see why. He was just so big and commanded the entire building. I'd read in the guidebook that his ears alone measured almost two feet. The giant limestone likeness lay on its back with its braided beard and signature cartouche proclaiming him Rameses II, Pharaoh. He looked so regal and important that we didn't say much as we walked around the statue.

"Shall we get a look from above?" Dad finally asked. I could tell that he was awed by the enormity of the stone form.

We all nodded and climbed a stairway leading to a balcony that gave us a different vantage point.

"He looks so peaceful," Kari commented. We all agreed.

After we left the building, we walked into an outdoor area with several smaller statues, including an alabaster sphinx. Much smaller than the Giza Sphinx near the Pyramids, the Sphinx of Memphis still weighed a hefty eighty tons, a sign told us.

I fell in love with him for some reason. Maybe it was the contrast of his whiteness to the brilliant green background vegetation that grabbed me. Whatever it was, I sat down on a bench near the lion-man, while the others, who weren't as taken by the statue as I was, continued to walk around.

It's a great day to be alive, I thought. The March sun was just comfortably warm, and as a heavenly breeze ruffled my hair, I felt a deep sense of peace as I breathed in the clean, fresh air. I decided to record the beauty and peace of the scene in my journal.

Dad, Susan, and Kari came back over to the

bench after I'd written a few paragraphs.

"Let's eat," Dad said, rubbing his hands together.

"The hotel fixed us a veritable feast," Susan put in.

When I looked at the graceful curve of the palm trees framing the statues from the distant past, I thought how perfect this spot would be for a picnic.

"Why don't we eat here," I suggested.

"It's as good a place as any," Dad said. Susan and Kari nodded.

They left me writing in my journal about the ancient Egyptian capital, whose heyday had been in the Old Kingdom, while they walked back to the car for the hamper.

Lower Egypt
Memphis

Memphis, my entry continued, *I don't know what to write about your past. What was it like when Menes built the first fortress way back at the very starting point of Egyptian history? No doubt you grew . . . and grew. Where are your elaborate temples now? Are the ghosts of your royalty in their jewels and gold still here? I looked around me again at how little was left. Gone,* I wrote, *and yet . . . and yet maybe less is more. Maybe for those with imagination, you still exist. You are a spirit, a feeling.*

When I looked up again to savor the quietude of the scene, I noticed Kari walking back to me, alone, with the picnic basket.

"Where are Dad and Susan?" I asked.

"Well, when we were getting out the hamper," she explained, "Mom looked at that area with the broken columns. The way she said it looked romantic, and the way your dad looked at her spoke volumes. I told them we'd meet them at the car in an hour. They took half the food."

"They're having a pretty good time, don't you think?"

"Yeah. That's why I made myself scarce."

It sort of surprised me that she'd been that perceptive, but I didn't say anything.

"I didn't really read that, you know," she said, pointing to my travel journal.

I nodded.

"I don't know why you'd think I would," she challenged.

I could think of a dozen reasons, actually, but I didn't want to get into her stupid behavior at home. Not here. Not now.

"Let's drop it and just enjoy the day," I suggested. "Isn't this a fantastic place?"

"Let's not. I want to know," she pressed, and something in her expression told me that she wouldn't be put off. Why couldn't we just eat?

I sighed.

"Kari, think."

"What's that supposed to mean?" she asked with a certain snippiness in her voice that really irritated me. It was so *Kari*.

"Let's just not get into it now," I said as I reached for the hamper. She pulled it away.

"Why do you always try to run away from things?" she asked.

What! She was trying to turn everything back on me. I just couldn't believe it. My sense of peace evaporated then, and all the anger I had bottled up for months started foaming inside me. Now she'd even tried to ruin this special place. I'd had it with her.

"All right, Kari. *Things* made me wonder if you'd read it. You know. Back home. The names you called me. The pictures on my locker. Making fun of me. Trying to trash my reputation. Don't you think that's cruel? That's why I wouldn't have put it past you to read my diary."

Was that look on her face real or fake? I couldn't believe she hadn't seen any connection between her behavior at home and my thinking she'd read my private thoughts.

"How could you have done those things, Kari? What did I ever do to you?"

"Mom married your dad," was all she said.

"So?"

"So, that makes you my stepsister. I never asked for a *handicap* in my family."

What! There was that awful name again. I hated it even more than I hated being called Boozy Beth. Ooh, I'd let that brat have it. I stared hard at her.

"Listen, Kari Quinn, and get this straight. People have things wrong with them—handicaps, if you will, or disabilities—but that doesn't make *them* 'handicaps.' I never asked to get sick when I was four years old. I never asked to have my hearing and balance screwed up. But it's what happened thanks to an illness called meningitis, and I can't change it. I'm Beth Antonia Langford, not a 'handicap,' and I have a personality and abilities just like everyone else does. I have feelings. I need to love and be loved like anyone else. Kari, I *bleed* just like you do."

How could I make her understand that people calling me names cut into the very heart of who I am? Why couldn't she accept me the way I am? Then I had it.

"What about your handicap?" I asked.

If she'd been quiet, that last question brought her

out of her trance.

"Me a handicap?" she said indignantly.

"No, I didn't call you a handicap. I said, 'What about your handicap?'"

"I don't have any. You're the one with the handicap. Do you have any idea how embarrassing it is to have you as a stepsister?"

"There! That's what I mean about your having a handicap, Kari. What's the matter with you deep down inside that you find me an embarrassment? Talk about embarrassment! What do you think it was like when I fell down the stairs at school, heard somebody calling me Boozy Beth, saw my tampon roll out of my purse right in front of Tom Edelman, and then saw you and those witchy friends of yours laughing your heads off?"

"Well, it was kind of funny, like a slapstick routine," she explained. She actually laughed at the memory of what had been so painful for me. I wanted to lunge at her and throttle her, but I just clenched my fists as I tried to keep myself together.

"It probably was," I finally admitted, "but that doesn't mean you're supposed to laugh at another person's expense. Slapstick is supposed to be funny. I'm not one of those old comedians stepping on a banana peel. What if that had been you? How would you have felt? Did you ever stop to think of that? Didn't you ever learn the Golden Rule?"

She had the nerve to turn things back onto me.

"It wouldn't be so bad if you didn't use your handicaps for attention."

Ooh . . . there she went again! She really knew how to press my buttons. I hated being accused of things like that.

"What's that supposed to mean?" I asked. She'd better have a good answer.

"You pretend you're deaf when you want to, yet

you're hearing me just fine now."

"I thought we covered that in the hotel room that night when you started talking to me and I didn't have my hearing aid on. Don't you remember I really couldn't hear?"

"Yeah."

"Well?"

"But in school you're teacher's pet. If you have so much trouble hearing, why don't you get a sign language interpreter? But no, Beth, you just sit up there in front for attention."

"Teacher's pet! There you go again. Why do you have to do that?" I asked.

"Do what?" She really didn't seem to know.

"Accuse me of things. So you think that if I got an interpreter it'd be—zippo, zappo—everything's rosy? It doesn't work that way, Kari. I'd get an interpreter if I were deaf and used sign language, but as you yourself pointed out, I hear pretty well with my hearing aid on. It doesn't take a brain surgeon to figure out that sitting up front helps because the sound is closer. Sometimes I can even lipread a little to help, but I have to be close for that, too. Do it for attention! I do it because I have to."

"Okay, okay, I hear you," she said. Then she changed the subject. Good. Maybe I'd put her in her place. "Listen," she continued, "we'd better eat something, or Mom and your dad will wonder."

"Yeah," I agreed. I'd forgotten all about eating. "They're essentially on their honeymoon. We owe it to them, if not to ourselves, not to fight."

"I don't think they've picked up on how we feel about each other," Kari said as she began opening the hamper. She took out two bottles of Gini soda as I reached in for some bread and cheese and an orange. There were even our favorite Oriental sweets.

"Maybe not," I said, "but isn't it taking a lot of

. . . .

148

energy to act in front of them? Kari, why do we even need to put on an act? Can't we work on being friends?" *Friends.* Did I really say that word?

She popped a grape into her mouth as I spread cheese onto my bread.

"Why would you even want to be friends with me? I'm the cruel one. Right?"

"I didn't say you were cruel. I said some of the things you did were cruel. Sometimes good people do bad things, you know."

"And you think I'm good?"

"Well, I don't even know. I'm willing to look for the good in you. But you have to do something too."

"What?" she asked skeptically.

"Don't try to sabotage us."

She looked out at the palms then. Was she considering what I'd said?

"Okay," she finally answered. Her eyes had gone down to her shoes, but fortunately she'd spoken into my good ear. Then she looked right at me and added, "I didn't read the journal, you know."

"All right, all right. I believe you," I told her with a little laugh.

Could it really be? Was this a truce at last? I had a strong hunch that it wasn't the end to our personal conflict, but the spirit of Memphis, it seemed, had worked its mystique. As we ate our lunch, our conversation shifted to Egypt. By the time Dad and Susan rejoined us, we were eager for the next stop.

The way from Memphis to Saqqara was short, so it was really weird the way the landscape changed abruptly from emerald lushness to sandy desert. How fitting, I thought, since Memphis had been the side where people had lived, while Saqqara had been their ancient burial grounds.

"It's so green on one side and brown on the

149

other," I commented. "It's as if a giant had drawn a line in the earth to mark the difference." I'd seen the American Southwest with its cacti and sagebrush and little desert flowers, but this was something else—just an ocean of sand with no visible living thing in it.

"It's forbidding to see what the lack of water does," Susan turned around to say. I liked the way she usually remembered to include me.

Then we grew silent as another famous Egyptian landmark rose before us. The Step Pyramid of Zoser looked like a giant sandstone wedding cake. I knew it wasn't as tall as Giza's Great Pyramid, and it had a different shape, but it was so old that it fascinated us all.

I quickly paged through the guidebook and learned that Imhotep had fashioned it in the 3rd Dynasty. Was I really seeing something four-and-a-half thousand years old? It really blew my mind.

We couldn't go inside the pyramid, but we looked closely at its six "steps" of great stone blocks, and enjoyed the nearby *mastabas*, which Granmary had told me were private Old Kingdom tombs. Of brick and stone with sloping walls and a flat roof, they had evolved into the step pyramid form and, eventually, into the true pyramid shape. They were really ancient.

After we'd had our fill of looking around Saqqara, we stopped at a carpet school on the way home. It was called a school, but it was sort of like a mini-factory where black-haired children sat several to a bench before upright looms as they tied knots. The upper part of the loom looked like hundreds of plain white threads, but the lower section had been magically transformed by the little fingers into the kinds of intricate designs we associate with Oriental carpets.

A little girl in a bright red-print floor-length dress and a hot pink scarf flashed me a smile. Then she asked for *piastres* by touching the palm of one hand with the forefinger of the other. Universal sign language, I thought. Since it wouldn't be fair to give her money and not the other children, I just smiled apologetically and shook my head. I wished I'd brought a lot of candy or something to pass around.

A man told us the children had to stop working in the carpet school when they were about ten, since their hands got too large to tie the knots right. They attended regular school for three or four hours a day and then worked on the looms for five more hours. If they hadn't looked happy, clean, and well-fed, I might have felt sorry for them.

We saw their rugs for sale in the next room. They were such beautiful colors, often of silk threads. Dad bought Susan a small one in shades of peacock, ruby, and topaz.

After the carpet school, it was time to start back to the hotel. As we rode along, I was looking off to my right, toward the canal, when Kari poked my arm and said, "Oh, look!"

The fiery ball of the sun was getting low and staining the sky the most exquisite orange-rose color. It would have been a beautiful sunset anywhere, but what made this one special was seeing the Pyramids of Giza outlined majestically against the colorful backdrop.

"It looks like something out of *National Geographic*," Kari said appreciatively. Everyone else was just as entranced by the postcard-perfect scene.

"Could we get out for a minute to watch?" I asked.

"I'll try," Dad told us. There was nowhere to pull over right then, but he found a spot a mile or so down the road.

The sun had sunk quite a bit in just that time. By the time we got out and watched, it hovered at the apex of one pyramid as the sky subtly changed hue. The pyramid trio—Cheops, Chephren, and Mycerinus—sat mutely dramatic against the blood-red sky.

"There it goes!" Kari exclaimed as the sun finally dipped behind them.

Quickly, they became black silhouettes against a background that was turning to violet.

I wanted to bottle the sunset moments and keep them forever.

Chapter Fifteen

"What's that blue thing over by the closet?" Kari asked as she went over to investigate.

We were so tired from the long, emotional day, plus a slow, many-coursed dinner on the way back from Saqqara, that we had slipped right into our pajamas after getting back to our room that night.

"I don't have any idea," I said as I watched her carry the long, skinny object back. The only thing that came to my mind was a ski pole wrapped in tissue paper, but Egypt was hardly ski country. I wrote off that idea.

"There's a card attached," Kari informed me. She gave me an odd look. "It has your name on it," she added after quickly flipping it over.

"My name?" I commented as I took the long item from her. "That's weird. Maybe it's something your mom bought that time we shopped. You know, when you and Dad were playing tennis."

"It's odd something she bought would be in our room, though."

"Yeah, you're right," I agreed.

"Well, open it, Beth."

"I'll open the envelope first." My name on it was in bold handwriting that I didn't recognize. I pulled out a square white card that read:

> *Dear Miss Langford,*
> *Please accept this gift to enhance your*
> *enjoyment of Upper Egypt. It belonged to my*
> *cousin, who no longer needs it.*
> *Best wishes,*
> *Asmie*

How curious, I thought as I handed the note to Kari to read.

"Asmie? Who's Asmie?" she asked after reading it.

"That Egyptian guy with the hose," I explained as I began working on the little strings tied around the long package.

"But isn't he old enough to be your—"

"Don't worry," I told her. "Yeah, he's pretty old, all right, so don't get any ideas. I have no idea what this is all about, but there's absolutely no romance."

I looked up at her for a moment. Was it my imagination, or did Kari Quinn actually seem a little protective of me just then? I couldn't help smiling a little as I undid the last knot.

"Here goes," I said, but I pulled the paper away slowly, not sure what I would find. As I did, I still wondered what Asmie could possibly be giving me. Then I had my answer.

"A cane!" I exclaimed, not too happily. Was this a joke of some kind?

"Wow, it's a pretty one," Kari said. "And it's not a cane, Beth, it's a walking stick. See how long it is?"

"Yeah." She was right. It was both long and pretty. Of some kind of black material, it had some gold squiggles up and down its length and a brass lotus blossom for a top. "It looks too nice. I don't know if I should keep it."

"It is unusual. Well, he wouldn't have given it to you if he hadn't wanted to. Besides, from the note, it sounds like it was his cousin's. Maybe it's a woman's stick and Asmie didn't want it."

"Maybe. And he did see me fall out there on the driveway."

"Well, that explains it. That's pretty thoughtful of him."

"It really is. I don't know how I feel about . . . oh, I don't know." Would she make something of it if I let her know that the idea of a cane sort of turned my stomach? Didn't old people use them?

Somehow, Kari picked up on what I hadn't said.

"It's a walking stick," she reminded me. "Lots of people use them. Here," she said, reaching for it, "let me demonstrate." She didn't make a parody at all. She used it as anyone might when hiking. "It makes sense for Upper Egypt. Isn't it sort of slopey by the tombs? And Karnak might have lots of rubble."

I took it back from her.

"Thanks," I told her. "I love it!" I decided. "I just hope Dad lets me keep it."

"He will."

The truce between Kari and me actually held pretty well for the rest of the time we had in Cairo before leaving for Luxor, and Dad did let me keep the walking stick. I was clumsy with it at first, but once I got the hang of it, I loved the secure feeling it gave me when I walked.

Unfortunately, Asmie was off work, and I never had a chance to thank him in person for the wonderful present. I hoped the note I left for him at the hotel's desk would do.

It might have been sad to leave Cairo, but we'd have an extra day there at the end of our trip, before catching the jet back home. And Upper Egypt beckoned. Upper Egypt! It was the place I'd wanted to see more than anywhere else in the world. And now I was on my way via Egypt Air.

Even though I had the window seat this time, except for a glimpse of the Pyramids as we took off, there wasn't a whole lot to see from the air. The Great Western Desert stretched on and on almost like the Atlantic Ocean had on our way over. Shortly before we landed, though, I saw how different this new area was. There were fields of sugar cane and other warmer latitude crops, for one thing, in a narrow band along the Nile. It also felt warmer when we got off the plane.

A stiffly formal little boy in a scarlet uniform greeted us at our hotel, and as we made our way down a long hallway to our room, again I was thankful for Asmie's gift. The walking stick really helped that falling-over feeling I often had in long corridors.

Our new room had pretty papyrus-print wallpaper and a weird-shaped little balcony set at an odd angle. We had a better view of the pool than of anything else. Then I leaned out and drew in my breath.

We did have a view! I could see just enough of the jutting mass of cliff across the Nile to unmistakably identify it as the fabled tomb area where King Tut's treasures had been found. "The Valley of the Kings!" I exclaimed as I positioned Kari just right so that she could glimpse it too. It gave her duck bumps, she said. Then she offered me the bed next to the bathroom.

The day was almost gone by the time we'd checked in, unpacked a little, and had a bite to eat.

It was when we were eating in one of the hotel's restaurants that we met Mrs. Brinion. She must have heard us talking and knew we were Americans.

"I hope you don't mind my asking," came her voice right into my good ear from the next table, "but what part of the States are you from?"

"Oh, hello," Susan said. Kari and I also greeted her.

"Our accents must be a dead giveaway," Dad laughed. The silver-haired woman, who was sitting at her table alone, nodded and chuckled along with him. I could see from her plate that she was just about finished with her dinner. Dad answered her question with, "We're from Oregon."

"Oh, Oregon," she said appreciatively. "What part are you from? I'm from Cincinnati, by the way."

"We're from Fir Grove, a suburb of Portland," I told her. Her face lit up.

"Fir Grove! My, what a small world. My daughter lives there," she said. She looked from me to Kari and back again. "I'll bet you girls go to Elston."

Kari and I nodded.

"I'm Dorothy Brinion," she told us. Dad introduced us all by name then, and I wondered how Kari felt about being the only Quinn among us Langfords.

"Are you traveling with a group?" Susan asked.

"No, dear," she said. "I'm here getting background for a novel I'm writing."

"How wonderful," Susan replied. Then, "Wait a minute. Dorothy Brinion? Are you the author of *Murder in York Minster Apse, Chambord Reverie,* and *The Delft Dilemma?"*

Mrs. Brinion blushed.

"Among others," she told Susan. Susan really warmed to that, and the two women began talking about some of Mrs. Brinion's books. Her name didn't ring any bells, but when I thought of the stacks of books in any library, it was no wonder.

"Is the one set in Egypt going to be a mystery, too?" Kari asked. Mrs. Brinion nodded and Kari went on with, "Oh, please tell us about it."

"Please do," I coaxed. I'd never met an author.

She smiled at Kari and me.

"In a nutshell," she explained, "my main character spots a man near the Pyramids of Giza who's a dead ringer for her late husband. The story involves a statue of the cat-goddess, a Bastet, and brings her here to Luxor."

"Uh oh. I bet he's not really dead," Kari said

when Mrs. Brinion paused.

"I'll bet that Bastet is the key," I put in.

"You could be right," she said with a twinkle in her eyes, "but now I can't tell you, can I, or it wouldn't be a mystery."

I wondered what it would be like to think your husband had died, only to find him alive in Egypt, of all places. Maybe that Bastet was an artifact he wanted to smuggle out of the country. Could people really do that with all of today's security? I supposed there were ways.

Susan, who had been listening carefully to one of her favorite writers, asked, "What's the title? I'll watch for it."

"That's still unsettled, Susan. One just hasn't come to me yet."

Susan nodded.

"Writing a novel must be an interesting process," Dad commented. He wasn't really into her kind of book and hadn't said much during the book talk.

"That it is," agreed Mrs. Brinion. Then she patted her totebag. "In fact, I'd better get cracking on that process. I need to go up to my room and check over the day's notes."

As she got up to leave, we told her it was nice to meet her.

"I couldn't agree more," she said. "I hope we'll see one another again."

"Bye," we chorused as she left.

We thought about going to the Sound and Light show at Karnak that night. It would be thrilling to see the huge temple complex all lit up, but in the end, we decided we wanted our first impressions of it to be in broad daylight. That seemed right. It was, after all, the jewel dedicated to *Amun-re*, the Egyptian sun god.

"Let's make it an early night," Dad suggested,

"and be rested for Karnak tomorrow."

The next morning, though, Susan had a touch of "pharaoh's revenge," the condition tourists often get. Since it didn't seem fair for the rest of us to go to Karnak the first time without her, Kari and I walked around the hotel shops and grounds while Dad stayed close to Susan. With that pink stuff she was taking, Susan might be fine by afternoon.

We were in a garden between the hotel and the Nile River, looking at all the different-colored bright flowers and the green, green grass and leaves.

"I don't know much about flowers," Kari commented.

"That reddish-purple one is bougainvillea," I told her as I pointed to a big bush that was ablaze with flowers. I'd seen them in California.

"It's really showy and pretty," Kari said. "And I like all the cheery little marigolds in the borders. At least I know those. I don't know what that red stuff next to them is, though, do you?"

"No, it's very different-looking."

"Yeah. I bet they have a lot of things here that we don't have at home."

"I'm sure they do," I agreed. I looked around at the profusion of plants. "As beautiful as this garden is, it's too bad it cuts off the view of the Nile. Can you really believe that's the *Nile* down there?"

"It's pretty unreal. I wonder if there are any crocodiles left in it," Kari mused.

"I know there used to be an awful lot of them, but the Aswan High Dam changed things. I don't think there are too many left in this part of the river."

"Well, as long as one doesn't decide to join us here, I don't care," Kari laughed. I guessed I didn't, either, but then again, maybe I did. I'd read that even though that dam had given the Egyptians the electricity they'd needed to modernize, its construction had been a double-edged sword, changing things like ancient flood patterns that had left certain areas very fertile once the water had receded. Now the right nutrients weren't in areas that had been great farming regions. So, maybe the crocodiles had been a good sign.

Kari walked over to a shrub with a little blue flower on it.

"Mom would love this. It's her favorite periwinkle blue color."

"I hope she gets better fast," I commented as I admired the bush.

"Me, too. Your dad is so good about taking care of her."

"Yeah."

"Does that bother you sometimes?" she asked.

"Bother me?"

"Uh huh."

"Well, I don't know if 'bother' is the right word, but it sort of hurts sometimes, Kari. Don't get me wrong, though. I think your mom's great, but sometimes it's just hard to see them so happy and remember the way Dad and my mom and I used to be a family. I just never thought my parents would split up." I remembered that Kari's parents were also divorced. "But you must know how that is."

"Sort of."

"What do you mean?"

"Mom and Dad got their divorce just before my second birthday," she explained, "so I don't remember us all being together."

So it had been just Susan and little Kari for all those years. Even though I wasn't that happy with my own father in some ways, memories of the good times with him washed over me. It was just countless little things, like the way he'd change his voice to different

· · · · · · · · · · · · · ·
160

characters as he read me bedtime stories, or the way he'd taken me to a hotel tearoom with a chandelier some Saturdays for cake and milk. I felt so sorry for Kari.

"Was it hard growing up without a dad?" I asked.

"Sometimes," she admitted, "but it wasn't that bad. I mean, I never had anything else to compare my life with. Mom and I were happy and did plenty of fun things. But I also did a lot with my dad."

"You did? That must have been hard to be in the middle when you were so little," I commented. For the first time, I wondered how a very young child would handle divorce, like all the fighting and the undercurrents between her parents. Even though I didn't understand what went on with my folks, at least I could intellectualize it a little. I knew it wasn't really about me.

Kari looked sort of puzzled.

"In the middle?" she asked. "Oh, you mean like you are with your parents?"

"Yeah."

"Well, it may come as a shock, but my parents are good friends. Dad and his wife even send my mom birthday cards."

"Birthday cards?" I laughed. "I'm sorry, Kari. It's just that I thought of my mom and dad just then. You know if she got one, it'd end up right in the wastebasket unopened. She did that with some flowers he sent."

"Not my parents," Kari said. "They even send each other Christmas presents and stuff like that."

"You mean your mom actually tolerates your dad's other wife?" I asked in amazement. I thought of the way Mom's voice dripped with venom whenever she referred to Susan as *that woman*. She wouldn't even say her name, so trying to picture any acceptance was impossible.

"Uh huh. That's what I mean. Mom likes Gail

and thinks she's good for Dad, and their boys are almost like Mom's nephews or something. We're all sort of extended family."

"I didn't know you have stepbrothers. How old are they?" Had Kari been weird with them, too?

"Kevin is nine, and Adam is six. And they're my *half* brothers."

"Oh, they're just little."

"They're really neat little kids. They live in Renton, Washington, but I see them several times a year."

"So you're not in the middle at all," I said, trying to picture it.

"No, and maybe you won't always be, either, Beth."

I rolled my eyes.

"I don't know, Kari. I love my mom and all, but she's really written Dad off."

All of a sudden, Kari walked a little closer to me.

"Left ear, right?" she asked. When I nodded, she leaned close to my ear and said, "Listen, I'm not trying to change the subject or anything, but is that man over by the door leading back into the hotel weird or what?"

When I shifted positions a little and casually looked over by the door, I saw a man in a brown suit lounging against the wall. He was smoking a cigarette. Was he staring at us, or was it only my imagination? Anyway, if that suit was weird in this place of casual, lightweight tourist clothes, the man's face was even more so. He looked familiar, like the Egyptians of old, with deep tea-colored skin, high cheekbones, and hollowed-out cheeks.

"He looks like Rameses II," I said. At that point, the man flipped his cigarette onto the pavement and stomped it out with his foot. Then he went back indoors and we forgot him.

"You were saying something about your mom writing your dad off," Kari said, getting back to our conversation.

"Yeah, she's really closed-minded about it. I wish I understood it better."

"Well, I dunno. Maybe since she's a public figure, getting divorced is embarrassing. Hurt pride can make people act funny. And if she really, deeply loved your dad, she must hurt an awful lot, way deep down inside."

Maybe Kari had something there. Maybe Mom's anger was really a defense mechanism to hide her hurt—maybe even to herself.

"That's logical," I told Kari.

"Well, just remember that for most people, time has a way of healing. She'll mellow out sooner or later."

"I hope you're right."

"Now, how about some *leban zabadi*? Don't you just love the way those words roll off your tongue?"

"Yeah, and I could really go for a dish," I seconded.

Then we walked into the hotel for the thick, creamy yogurt we'd tried for the first time just yesterday.

Chapter Sixteen

Susan did feel better that afternoon, so the trip to Karnak was on!

"Did you remember to put on sunblock?" Susan asked as we waited in the lobby for the shuttle bus. Dad, Kari, and I wore shorts and T-shirts, but Susan had on a sundress and carried a long-sleeved gauze blouse over one arm for protection from the intense Upper Egypt sun.

We nodded in answer. I'd really slathered mine on.

"We have our hats, too," Kari told her. Susan smiled, but I thought she still looked a little under-the-weather.

"Are you sure you're well enough to go?" I asked. "We don't mind waiting another day."

"I'm fine," she told me. "I don't think I can wait another day," she added with a wink. Then, "Oh, there's Mrs. Brinion."

When I looked up, Mrs. Brinion, wearing a big floppy sunhat, was just coming into the hotel.

"Hello," she called as she waved at us.

"Hi, Mrs. Brinion," Kari called out. The rest of us waved at the writer, who carried her large totebag. When she came over closer, I could see a notebook inside, plus a couple of books.

"A working morning?" Dad said.

"That's right, Bruce. I like to do it in the cool of the day. It's getting hot out there."

"I hope not too hot. We're just on our way to Karnak," Dad told her.

"Smart move," she said. "It's so crowded with

tour groups in the mornings. Even though it's heating up, it's a dry heat, and fortunately there are spots of shade within the temple complex."

"Oh, good," Susan said.

"Why, Beth, what a beautiful walking stick," she said then as she moved closer to me. "May I see it?"

As I handed it to her, I said, "Thank you. It was a gift."

"A unique one," she said as she turned it over and over to examine the golden squiggles. "I like this lotus on the head." She handed it back and looked from one to the other of us before adding, "Good. I see you all have hats. You might also want to take some bottled water."

We thanked her for the reminder, and as Mrs. Brinion told us it was time for her nap and began to walk to her room, Dad bought some water for us to take along.

I was so excited on the bus to Karnak that I could hardly stand it. I knew lots of hieroglyphic-inscribed columns and temples were left. Unlike Memphis, there would be a lot of tangible evidence of the grandeur that had been. I closed my eyes for a few moments and imagined high-cheeked pharaohs and their women bedecked with huge collars made of gold, carnelian, and lapis lazuli. In my mind, I heard a strange, lost language and felt the deep mystery of such a long-ago past.

Then I opened my eyes.

"Oh, there's the First Pylon!" I said in wonder as I caught my first glimpse of the huge towers at the entrance to the temple area. As my anticipation mounted, the double towers grew ever-bigger as the bus lumbered down a tree-lined avenue before dropping us off near a small booth where Dad bought our entrance tickets.

"I guess we walk across that footbridge," he said

as he handed us each a ticket. They were pale gold with brown stamps on them. "Let me take a few pictures of you before we cross over," he added.

Then we were on our way, moving closer to the massive First Pylon, and I felt as though I were moving in a wonderful dream. I crossed the footbridge and stood in the Avenue of Rams, where stone statues of rams were lined up on either side of the walk.

"Oh, isn't that cute?" Susan said as she pointed to some of the rams. At first I didn't know what she meant. Then I saw two real black goats munching on the tufts of grass at the bases of two of the stone figures. Something caught in my throat at the sight. *Granmary*, I thought. She would have gotten such a kick out of the combination of common, ordinary goats and the very regal-looking stone rams.

I'm not going to cry, I told myself. Remembering Granmary, instead, with the smile she wanted, I looked through the opening between the great towers. The scale of what I saw boggled my mind. I knew Karnak was really big—something like two hundred acres—but I couldn't believe it when I looked down the long, long expanse that went to and through the Great Court, the Great Hypostyle Hall, and on to the Great Temple of Amun.

"Incredible!" I said.

"These towers are so huge," Kari remarked, still focused upon them. I looked back at their bulk.

"The First Pylon is Ethiopian," Susan reminded us. Something about the way she said it echoed her grandmother, and it made me feel almost as if Granmary were with us at Karnak, her favorite place in the world. It was a very good, peaceful feeling.

"Those walls of the towers are a good forty-five to fifty feet thick," Dad commented in awe as we passed through the opening between them.

"You can still see the ramps behind this unfinished south tower," I said as I pointed to some ancient mud brick ramps for hauling stones. Everyone looked and nodded.

Then we were in the Great Court with its colonnades on both sides, more statues of rams, and temples and chapels galore in and around the huge open space of the court.

"It's so big," I said.

"Awesome!" Kari exclaimed. "It'd take hours just to see everything in the Great Court."

"I agree," Dad said. "In fact, maybe we should do that kind of exploring on a subsequent visit and make this a self-styled mini-tour. You know, to get an overview of Karnak." I think he was a little worried that Susan's trouble might come back, but it sounded like a good idea anyway. The temple complex was too big to see in-depth at one time.

"That sounds good to me," I told him. Susan and Kari agreed.

If the Great Court had been impressive, the Great Hypostyle Hall really blew our minds. As we entered the largest single chamber of any temple in the world, the exclamations went around:

"I can't believe this!" Susan said.

"Wow!" Kari put in.

"Astounding!" Dad commented.

For a moment, I just stood there, frozen in delight and wonder as I saw the enormous roomful of gigantic columns. One hundred thirty-four of them, I thought in awe. Then I walked forward and immediately felt dwarfed.

"It's like standing in a reddish-brown stone woods," Susan said as she entered the column area.

Dad looked up at the sky and remarked, "It took all sixteen rows of them to hold the long-gone roof over an area larger than a football field."

I missed any other comments then, since the columns seemed to soak up sound like huge cylindrical sponges. I didn't mind at all. It was time for looking.

The twelve largest columns along the hall's central aisle soared sixty-nine feet high and were a fat thirty-three feet around. Huge open-flower lotuses topped them. As I craned my neck to look up at them, again I had that feeling that Granmary was with us. "A hundred people, Beth," she had told me. "That's how many a tour guide said could stand in each eleven-foot-high stone flower."

I could believe it!

The other hundred twenty-two columns had closed-bud capitals, or tops, but even though they were smaller than the central ones, they were no less impressive. There were just so many of them.

As I used my walking stick to steady myself among the forest of giant columns, a delicious play of light and shadows fell throughout the roofless hall, since the columns made bands of darkness across the blaze of Egyptian sun. Where the light shone on the columns, I saw wonderful hieroglyphic inscriptions. I stopped to look at a few. There were some wavy lines that probably represented water. And an *udjat*, or stylized eye. I wished I could read them. Maybe I should become an Egyptologist, I thought, as I looked at symbol after symbol of the ancient language. I was so intent upon looking that a sudden sound nearly startled me out of my shoes.

"Yikes!" came the voice. A moment later Kari appeared. She'd been making her way around the same column. We both jumped.

"Wouldn't this be an awesome place to play hide-and-seek?" I said.

"Cool!" she said, nodding emphatically.

At the edges of the hall were great stone reliefs of carved symbols that told wonderful stories of ancient Egypt. Even though I couldn't read hieroglyphics, I could make a little of these out because they were carvings of people and familiar things. The one of Seti I on the north side, for example, had the pharaoh's inscribed likeness offering incense or something before entering the temple and kneeling before Amun.

Finally, we'd had our fill of the Great Hypostyle Hall for one day and moved on.

"It was nice and cool in there," Kari remarked as we went back out into full sunlight.

Dad shepherded us along a wonderland of more columns, temples, statues, and reliefs. There were symbols everywhere: the lotus to signify Upper Egypt, and the papyrus to represent Lower Egypt, and the double crown, or *pschent*, that symbolized the union of Lower and Upper Egypt. Pharaohs of the united kingdom had worn the crown.

Amun was alive and well at Karnak if the sun's intensity was any indication. I noticed that it was getting to Susan more than to the rest of us, and near the granite pillars by the Hall of Records, Dad finally insisted that Susan call it a day.

"Do you think we could stay here longer and look around some more?" Kari asked.

"We have that shuttle bus schedule and can catch one back," I said.

"That sounds fine with me, Bruce," Susan told my father. She was leaning against a wall and obviously felt terrible, but she managed to smile at Kari and me as she added, "I don't want to dampen your fun."

"Don't worry about that, Susan. We can always come back another day," I said.

"Yeah, Mom," Kari put in.

Dad thought about it. Then he said he guessed

we could stay, as long as we kept together.

"Take care," I told my stepmother.

"Get better fast, Mom."

Then they were gone.

Kari and I ambled all over for about an hour before we decided a soft drink would taste good. Our map showed a rest area near the Sacred Lake.

It was when I looked around trying to orient myself that I noticed a man in an old-fashioned, baggy brown suit that looked out of place. He wasn't staring at us or anything, but when I saw those old, old Egyptian features again, a little mental shadow passed over the bright sunny day.

"Psst, Kari," I whispered.

"Yeah?"

"Over to your left. Brown Suit!"

"Huh?"

"That man from the hotel garden. I thought I saw him earlier today, too, but I told myself it wasn't the same guy."

"Weird," Kari said, but I wasn't sure if she was just humoring me.

"It has to be a coincidence," I decided.

"Well, this is a major tourist attraction," she said. "But I'll keep my eyes peeled."

When we looked again, the man in the brown suit was nowhere in sight.

"Thanks," I told her. "Let's get those drinks."

As we neared the Sacred Lake, we passed a giant granite scarab beetle, the symbol of the rising sun. I remembered Granmary telling me that small versions of the bug had been placed on mummies in the position of the dead person's heart. I touched my ring.

"This is really cool," I said as I walked around the carving.

Kari wasn't looking at it.

"There's the lake up there," she said. Well, Granmary had said Kari didn't like bugs, so I reluctantly moved on without further comment.

If the rest of Karnak had been better than my wildest dreams, the Sacred Lake was almost disappointing. Maybe it was just the way the late afternoon light hit it, but it looked kind of stagnant and ordinary. The small bazaar at the water's edge also did little to suggest a sacred image.

We walked into the open-air refreshment stand, bought drinks, and then took them over to a wooden table and chairs.

"Mmm, this tastes wonderful," I commented as I sipped mine.

Kari was drinking hers, too, but she was just staring out over the lake.

"Tired?" I asked. She only shrugged her shoulders. I waited a minute or two and tried again with, "Your mom will be okay once she gets some rest."

"I know," she said. Her voice was so flat. She was in some kind of a mood.

As I saw all the postcards for sale near the lake, I decided to give it one more try. Kari loved to send them to everybody she'd ever met.

"They have some great cards over there," I told her, pointing to the shore. I'd never known Kari to bypass a good postcard stand.

"Why don't you just shut up?" she snapped.

Shut up? What had I done? Things had been going so well between us, and now it was almost like the Kari from home again.

"Kari, what's wrong?" I asked.

Her only answer was to get up and start running back the way we had come. What in the world? Then all of a sudden, I had a hunch what had changed Kari's mood. I set down my cup and went after her, but it was

....
171

at my own slower speed, and she'd gotten quite a way ahead of me by the time I finally caught up with her beside the giant scarab beetle.

Her back was to me, but I could still see her shoulders shaking. Was Kari crying? I'd guessed that the stone bug had reminded her of the ring her great-grandmother had given to me, but whatever was happening to Kari now seemed to go deeper than just a piece of jewelry, I thought, as I heard a terrible sob come from her.

"Kari?"

" . . . leave . . . -lone," she said, talking into the beetle rather than to me.

For a few moments, I was torn between leaving her and staying. Then I thought of Matt and how we'd had to face certain issues before moving on, and I knew it was time Kari and I had this talk. I moved in a little closer to her.

"I'm not going," I said.

She spun around angrily, and I could see from her red eyes and blotchy mascara that she'd definitely been crying her eyes out.

"Oh, you! Why do you have to be like that?" she said with what looked like pure exasperation. She clenched her fists.

"Like what?" I asked, genuinely perplexed.

"Like Beth Langford, that's what."

"Maybe it's because that's who I am," I told her softly.

"Yeah, that's the trouble," she all but spat out.

"What's the trouble?" I prodded. She seemed to be talking in riddles. But Kari either wouldn't, or couldn't, explain. Some instinct told me not to let it go. I walked even closer and invited, "Tell me what's wrong."

She looked into space as she told me, "It's none of your business." I saw a rivulet of tears on her cheeks.

"Here," I told her, handing her a tissue from my pocket.

"I don't want it."

"Oh, come on. Your mascara's going to ruin that T-shirt." She wiped the back of her hand across her cheeks, and when it came back black, she must have realized that her makeup really was making a big mess. She took the tissue.

"Thanks," she said as she blotted her face.

"Look," I told her, "I'm not trying to butt in, but I think I know why you're crying. It's Granmary, isn't it?"

She didn't answer at first, but a new flood of tears gushed out at the mention of Granmary's name. I waited while she calmed back down a little.

"Yeah . . . yeah," she faltered. "I just . . . well . . . I just miss her so much."

"Me, too. This was her favorite spot in, I think, the entire world."

"Yeah," Kari agreed, but the word came out as a little squeak.

I wished I knew what was going through Kari's mind. Maybe it was still the ring, partly. I loved it myself, but would it help if I gave it to Kari? In this special place of Granmary's, it was obvious that Kari was missing her achingly. I had thought of her, too, and been on the verge of tears myself, but then my reaction had changed to a sense of peace and even happiness at the memory of my octogenarian friend. Kari, though, just seemed to feel the sadness and loss. Maybe the ring would be like a spiritual bandage and heal the sting just a little. I twisted it off my finger. It had grown tight in the heat of the sun, but I finally got it off.

"Here," I told Kari. "Maybe if you put this on, you'll feel better."

She stared at it and seemed neither pleased nor

angry at my offer. Then she shook her head.

"No, it's yours. Please put it back on." She watched as I did and added, "The ring . . . it won't help."

"It's true. It won't bring her back. But, I don't know, Kari, somehow I feel like she's here with us, in this place she loved."

For some reason, that only made the tears start again.

"Me, too," she said through them. "But the difference between us, Beth, is that I don't like it. It's like she's haunting me."

"Haunting you? If she is, I know it's in the best of ways. Kari, she loved you so much."

Her reaction to that totally surprised me. She blew her nose, wiped away her tears again, and then she impaled me with her blotchy eyes.

"How dare you say that! Do you mean to tell me how my own great-grandmother felt about me? How presumptuous, Miss Goody Two-Shoes."

She was calling me names again! I couldn't believe it.

"Why do you resent me so much?" I asked. What had I done to her? She looked like she wanted to charge and scratch my eyes out.

"Oh, you . . . you were there and I wasn't," she said.

"Do you mean at your great-grandmother's?"

"That's right."

"I told you before that I really liked her, Kari. I enjoyed being with her." I remembered as I spoke how Kari had rarely been around her and, especially, how Granmary had thought for a moment in the hospital that I was Kari. I'd seen how disappointed she was when she realized I wasn't. It was hard to forgive Kari for letting her down that way. And then I blurted out, "Why weren't you there, anyway?"

She stared at some point on my shoulder with the weirdest look. Something strange crossed her face then. It looked like total disgust—maybe even hatred—but the emotion didn't seem directed at me.

"Why wasn't I there?" she asked. "Because I'm a crumb, Beth. I'm a total crumb. I was too busy for her, too into my own things. Still, I knew she was getting really old. I couldn't stand the thought of losing her. It just made me stay away even more. Then when I stayed away, I felt guilty, and it got harder and harder to go. Beth, I'm a terrible person. I felt *mad* at her for getting old, and I felt scared when I thought of her dying. She'd just always been there, you know."

Kari stopped for a breath and then continued.

"Why did I do that? Why did I shut her out of my life like that? I'm not a baby. I know people get old and die. I even volunteer at a hospice. I see it happen. It makes me sad, but it also makes me feel good to help those people by reading to them or running errands or just listening. Why didn't I listen to my own great-grandmother while I had the chance? I'm just a total crumb!"

The tears came again, and this time she really shook with grief and, I realized now, guilt.

I walked over to her and gently pushed her toward a place to sit down. After we sat, I let her cry it out, handing her a fresh tissue now and then. When she got the hiccups, I handed her the bottle of water.

"Drink some of this," I told her. She took a swig and held her breath. It didn't work the first time, but it did have the effect of easing her terrible sobbing.

"Thanks," she finally told me as she handed back the bottle.

How could I help her? I wondered. I wished I knew more about grief and guilt and stuff like that—more about *life*—but I could only blunder along and hope I'd hit on something to help.

"Kari," I told her, "you remember when we were talking about divorce in the hotel garden. Well, I didn't really know divorced couples could be friends like your parents are. I thought they were all like mine. The point I'm trying to make is that feelings and how we deal with them . . . well, that's pretty complicated stuff. There are different ways to deal with any situation. We seem to act as we need to. Some people, when someone is old or sick or something, need to be around, not just for the other person but for themselves. For some reason, you needed to back away from Granmary. It was your way of coping."

"But what she must have thought! I feel like she's watching me and shaking her finger at me or something."

"Don't be too hard on yourself. She was a very wise woman. I'll bet she had it all figured out," I told her.

"It wasn't that I didn't care."

"I understand that now. Is the guilt you felt for staying away, along with my going, why you did those things to me back home?" I asked.

"That's part of it," she admitted. "You were everything I wanted to be with Granmary."

"Again, don't be too hard on yourself, Kari. My relationship with her was a lot different than yours. Remember, you were her real relative. She'd known and loved you all your life. I only knew her for a matter of months. I loved her, yes, but my involvement wasn't anywhere near as deep as yours. Even so, I had a bad time when she died."

"How did you get over it?" she asked.

"I don't know that I have. She's really the first person I've ever lost through death. I know she had a long, wonderful life and all, but sometimes I feel like crying when I think of her not being there anymore."

"Yeah, but we're really crying for ourselves. It's selfish. I hate myself for it."

I thought of Matt's words: *You can't just feel the void of loss and celebrate. Feel the loss, be sad that she's gone, and then you're ready to move on to the point of celebrating her life.*

Kari's situation was a lot more complicated than mine, but I wanted to help her as Matt had helped me.

"Crying may be selfish," I told her, "but some types of selfishness are positive. Sometimes we have to think of ourselves, go into ourselves that way, in order to heal. I didn't come to that realization easily myself, you know."

"What do you mean?" she asked.

"Well, Granmary talked to me in the hospital and asked me to remember her with smiles, so when I finally cried, I felt almost like I was letting her down. I felt really crummy. But someone I love made me see that Granmary hadn't meant for me to stop being human. She'd meant for me to celebrate her life with smiles *after* the tears."

I paused and looked at Kari. She was really listening, and fortunately, other tourists weren't in our immediate area.

"Kari, don't ever hate yourself for loving or for being human." I paused a moment and then paraphrased some of Matt's words as I went on with, "It's okay to be sad that she's gone, it's okay to address your guilt—get help from your mom or someone if you can't handle it on your own—but know things will get better. Then you will be ready to celebrate Granmary's life and remember the good times you had with her happily, without all that baggage."

"Do you think so?" she asked with what sounded like a glimmer of hope.

"I'd be willing to bet on it."

Chapter Seventeen

Upper Egypt

*Today I'm going to the Valley of the Kings
in the ancient Necropolis of Thebes, across the
Nile from present-day Luxor. What will it be like
to walk into the many-chambered tomb of a
pharaoh whose mummy had been put there to rest
"for all eternity"? Will I smell the dust of the
ages?*

A delicious shiver ran through me as my pen
stopped on the journal page and I envisioned dark
passages and hieroglyphic texts on the walls, telling
stories of the pharaoh's life. Then for some reason I
thought of Matt. I started writing again.

*Matt, I wish you could be going there with
me, but then, it's funny, because I find myself so
often wishing you were seeing this or that with
me. I could tell you that I'm just a little scared to
go to this ancient burial place, and you wouldn't
even laugh at me. It's not that I think the
mummies still walk—it's not ghosts—so I guess
it's thinking back to what it must have been
like when they took the dead person's heart and
other organs out, embalmed him, and wrapped
him in layer upon layer of bindings before
sealing him away forever in nested coffins. In
an eerie way, it's almost as if I can project, only
I'm alive as the mummy wrappings go on and cut
my breathing, and I'm still alive as the final clink*

of the great sarcophagus holding my coffins becomes the last thing I hear.

When something tapped my shoulder I jumped.

"Eek!" I exclaimed. Then when I realized that I'd spooked myself writing and that it was just Kari, I broke out laughing.

"I was just laughing at myself," I told her. "I was writing in my journal about the tombs, and one thought led to another. It's funny how those old mummy movies stick with you."

"Boris Karloff isn't going to be in any of the tombs today," she said, but she wasn't making fun of me.

"I know. Oh, Kari, tombs of pharaohs! It sort of blows your mind," I said. Then I thought of her grief yesterday at Karnak and our talk. "Kari, this trip isn't going to be too hard on you, is it? I mean, going into *tombs*?"

"I'll just have to sort of play it by ear," she told me. "I don't think so."

"Well, if it starts to get to you because of Granmary and you need to talk, let me know," I offered.

"Thanks," she told me. She seemed okay.

After I'd helped Kari dry her tears at Karnak the day before, we had looked at the sun, which was getting low, and decided it was time to look for the shuttle back to the hotel. Since we were early for the bus, we walked over to a little souvenir shop just outside the temple complex, where rows of proud-looking stone cats— *Bastets*, I remembered Mrs. Brinion calling them—were lined up in one of the windows. They weren't expensive copies, but something about them appealed to me, and I bought a greenish one for Mom.

On the way back to the hotel, Kari said something I didn't hear.

"What?" I asked.

"Are you going to say anything about today?" she questioned.

"Not if you don't want me to."

"Thanks. I'll talk to Mom about it sooner or later."

"Good," I told her. I didn't like to think of Kari hurting, keeping things bottled up, and being eaten away with guilt.

We hadn't said anything more about our emotional afternoon.

Now in the hotel room, she brought me back to the present.

"The reason I tapped you before was to say that we'd better get down to the breakfast room soon."

I looked at my watch and said, "Yeah." We were leaving early to beat the heat.

Susan looked fine at breakfast, I was relieved to see.

"I feel a hundred percent better," she told us.

"Good," Kari and I said together. I noticed that Susan and Dad were just about finished with breakfast already.

"We got here a few minutes early," Dad said. "I hope you don't mind that we ate."

"I was famished," Susan explained. Last night, Kari and I had eaten dinner with Dad while Susan was still resting. Maybe she'd never eaten dinner.

"Don't worry about it," I told her. "I'm just glad your appetite is back."

"Yeah, Mom. I know how much you've been wanting to go across the river. We're sorry if we were a little late. We got to talking."

"We still have plenty of time," Susan assured us.

Mrs. Brinion breezed into the room just at Kari and I began eating. When Dad asked her to join us, she nodded and dropped her totebag and big sunhat off at our table before helping herself at the buffet.

"Are you off on an excursion today?" Dad asked, nodding at her sunhat, as she sat down.

"I'm off to Abydos and Dendera. I'm working a Seti I aspect into my book," she explained.

"You're up early yourselves," she noted.

"We're going to the Valley of the Kings," I told her.

Mrs. Brinion finished chewing a piece of roll before commenting. "Oh, what a fabulous place. You will all enjoy it enormously. Forgive me if I gobble my breakfast. My bus leaves in just a few minutes." She took another bite.

"Don't think anything of it," Susan told her.

Mrs. Brinion took a few sips of freshly-squeezed orange juice and said, "I overslept. I went to the Sound and Light spectacular at Karnak last evening. For the most part, it's a walking tour, you know, and as wonderful as the narrated history and all those dramatic lighting effects were, it was tiring."

"You look as fresh as the proverbial daisy," Dad told her.

"Thank you, Bruce. I do feel fine. And if you go to the Sound and Light, I highly recommend going by horse-and-carriage."

"That sounds like fun," Kari commented.

"We'll remember that," Susan added.

"Tell me your impressions of Karnak," Mrs. Brinion requested of Kari and me. "I'll eat while you talk," she laughed.

Kari and I, who were also still eating, traded off describing our favorite spots. I watched Kari for signs of sadness when she spoke of the temple complex, and I was glad to see that she spoke with interest untinged by emotional undercurrents. She'd been so upset.

Mrs. Brinion had been listening to us with great

interest. As she tipped her cup for what looked like the final sips of coffee, I said, "Let us know how you like Abydos and Dendera."

"That I will. And now, friends, I must run. Thank you for asking me to join you."

"The pleasure was ours," Dad told her. And then she was off.

Armed with sunblock, bottled water, and our hats, we left the hotel for the boat dock after breakfast. As we crossed the Nile by steamer, I watched the mass of rock cliffs grow larger as we neared the other side of the river. The Necropolis of Thebes, like other ancient Egyptian tomb places, was on the west bank—the dead side.

When the boat pulled up to the dock, though, it looked anything but dead. There must have been twenty-five or thirty tour buses.

I used my walking stick to steady myself as I got off the steamer. We passed a man in a white *galabia* hawking souvenirs. Bastets must be popular in this area, I surmised. The yellow-toothed man tried his best to sell us some little two-inch high versions, but Dad moved on and bought the coupons we needed to get into the necropolis.

Our bus was totally modern and air-conditioned, and we had a great view as we rode through an awesome pebbly desert with cliffs. The landscape was so totally inhospitable that it was hard to imagine ancient workers carving out tomb chambers and decorating them in this lonely place. How many had died of heatstroke? We were lucky not to be there in high summer, since the steep, rocky terrain was unshaded except, I guessed, for within the tombs themselves.

Our tour began in a section of the tomb area called the Valley of the Queens, where we walked through the Tomb of Queen Titi and then the many chambers of Queen Nefertari's. In one of the tombs, the guide briefly turned off the lights and cast us into pitch darkness. Maybe he had warned the others, but I hadn't heard him and was totally unprepared.

"Kari!" I called out. Even with the walking stick and a cold stone wall as touchstones, I felt like I was going to fall over in the sudden blackness.

I felt her grab my arm to steady me.

"Spooky!" she said.

"Yeah, as dark as a tomb. No pun intended." My laugh was sort of forced. It was such a total, absolute blackness that I couldn't see even one inch in front of me. It had a smothering effect.

Then I felt Kari's grip tighten as a woman screamed.

"I don't like this!" Kari exclaimed with panic in her voice.

"Me either." I felt the cold of the tomb seeping into me and shivered.

Just as I started to say I wished they'd turn the lights back on, they went on and nearly blinded us in contrast to the utter blackness of the moment before. Kari let go of my arm, and we both noticed a red-faced woman: the embarrassed screamer, no doubt. But our heart rates had been up there, too, and I sympathized with her.

Back in the bus, we chugged our way to the temple complex of Deir el-Bahri, built in the New Kingdom reign of Queen Hatshepsut.

"Isn't that magnificent?" Susan commented as we got out of the bus and looked at its three terraces linked by stone ramps. The whitish sandstone temple looked so dramatic against the steep, honey-colored cliffs, out in the middle of nowhere. We took pictures before climbing the first ramp.

As I struggled up it, I silently thanked Asmie once again. I couldn't have made it without my walking stick.

Dad commented on the temple dogs. Sturdy and medium-sized, they were almost the same color as the tall walls of rock in the background.

It was a do-it-yourself tour, but now and then we caught up with a major tour group and the rest of them listened in a little.

"I love these columns," Kari said.

"They're really different," Dad put in.

As we walked around them, their cow-headed capitals looked down at us. They looked sort of friendly.

"Hathor," Susan said. "The cow-headed goddess."

Although we passed beautiful reliefs in the Chapel of Anubis, the jackal-headed god, and other fascinating artwork, it was weird and sad that Queen Hatshepsut's name and likeness had been chiseled away or otherwise erased.

"Was it tourists?" Kari asked no one in particular.

"I wouldn't put it past them," Dad said. It was true that we'd seen names of modern-day people carved into beautiful columns and walls at places like Karnak. I didn't know what got into people to do something like that. Who cared if they'd been there, and what right did they have to deface something so old and beautiful?

Susan and I knew from Granmary that it wasn't tourists this time, though.

"No," she told them. "It wasn't tourists this time. It was politics." A guide and a flock of twenty or so people were coming toward us. Susan must have caught something he said. "Oh, he's telling the story now. Why don't we listen in?"

Of course I couldn't hear the guide, but I remembered the ancient stepfamily drama. Hatshepsut, the daughter of Tuthmosis I, had married her stepbrother,

Tuthmosis II. She acted as regent on behalf of Tuthmosis III, her stepson, before becoming Queen in her own right. After her death, though, her stepson became sole ruler and erased her name and likeness wherever he could. Judging from the pits in the walls and things, he'd done a pretty good job.

"You didn't miss anything," Susan said of the guide's narration. "Granmary told the story better." I smiled at her.

By the time we went back out, it was getting pretty hot, and we drank bottled water back on the bus on the way to the Valley of the Kings.

Of the sixty-odd discovered tombs, some were closed to the public for restoration or other reasons. The ones that were open offered a visual picnic of passageways adorned with priceless artwork, burial chambers where mummies had rested, and series of interconnected rooms whose size and number within a tomb indicated the pharaoh's importance in life.

"Stop," Dad said at one point. "I want to get your picture in front of the sign behind you."

When I turned to look at it, I read: TOMB OF TUTENCHAMUN NO 62. *King Tut!*

We took turns standing in front of the sign near the entrance to the famous tomb discovered in 1922 by Howard Carter. "The find of the century," it had been called.

It was push and shove as we got close. Dad had to leave his camera with an attendant, since flashbulbs damage some types of artwork. They weren't taking any chances with this fabled tomb. Two men debated about whether or not I could take my walking stick, but in the end, they let me go in with it.

They didn't let people just wander around. We got lumped together with an English-speaking tour group.

Kari said something I couldn't hear. The din of voices was like a bee buzzing in my hearing aid.

Howard Carter had walked down sixteen steps that led to his amazing find. I was disappointed that we didn't get to walk down the actual stairs. A new stairway had been built over the originals to accommodate the heavy foot traffic, but I felt satisfied when I spotted the ancient sixteen steps below.

As we walked along a rather nondescript passage, the guide spoke.

Dad drew up to me and said something. I think he offered to relate the guide's words, but the acoustics in the stone passageway were terrible.

"I can't hear you, Dad. You go ahead with Susan."

"Okay," he mouthed.

As we flowed ahead with the group, I thought the guide might be telling them that "Tut," the son-in-law of Akhenaten, had died at eighteen or nineteen. Younger than Matt, I thought. Although he had been only minor royalty, the things from his tomb had still been the most valuable find of the kind ever made in Egypt. When I remembered the gold and other fabulous treasures I'd seen from this tomb in the Egyptian Museum, I wondered what the finds from a major tomb, like Rameses II's, would have been like. So many of the tombs were plundered in long-ago times.

We walked through a doorway and then went down a narrow passage about twenty-five feet long. At the end of the tunnel, we came to another doorway that led us into an antechamber. I looked hard. It was here that Carter had found a magnificent collection of six to seven hundred items that included clusters of alabaster vases, parts of chariots, animal-sided couches, fabulous jewelry, beaded sandals, and the dazzling golden throne. Everything the ancients had thought Tut needed for his journey into the afterlife had been here. The room seemed too small to have held such a vast array of items.

The crowd was moving again, very slowly. My heart began beating faster as I realized the tomb chamber was just off to the side. Darn my shortness, I thought. I couldn't see over the others, and it was hard to be patient as we only inched along. From the hush, I knew we were getting close to what everyone wanted to see most.

Then the crowd thinned a little and I walked up to a railing. There it was! Even though I knew it would be there, I sucked in my breath, almost as if in surprise, for right in front of me, only feet away was a stunning sight.

In the space beyond the railing was a sarcophagus of yellowish crystalline sandstone lavishly covered with religious texts and scenes. There were figures of winged goddesses on its corners. Even though I couldn't see King Tut's mummy, I knew it was inside the sarcophagus. It might have been disappointing to have it all hidden away like that, but somehow it made it more thrilling. It was where the boy-king belonged.

I didn't get to look for long. The crowd oozed around me. I traded appreciative looks with Dad, Susan, and Kari. Then we moved along and it was over.

It was very hot when we got back outside.

"That was a moving experience," Susan commented. Kari and I agreed emphatically. Dad was getting his camera back and joined us near the entrance to the tomb.

"How would everybody like a cold drink?" Dad asked.

"I could go for one," Kari answered.

"Me too," I put in. Then we walked over to a near-by rest-house and were lucky enough to find a tiny table.

"Tomb dirt!" I said almost reverently as I looked at a smudge on the leg of my khaki pants. "I don't ever want to wash it off."

Susan and Dad laughed. Kari was busy looking down at her own slacks.

"Oh, good," she said. "I've got some too!"

As we enjoyed our drinks, we talked about the things we'd seen.

"I see why they send us over in the morning. It's really heating up," Susan said, "although it isn't bad in this shade."

"Are you still feeling okay?" I asked.

"Never better," she said with a smile.

Kari was lost in thought. Did she need to talk about Granmary again?

"Do you care if Kari and I go on ahead over to the bus loading area?" I asked.

Susan and Dad looked at each other.

"Why, no, that's fine," he said. "Give us about fifteen more minutes, and we'll be on our way. It feels so good to sit down."

"I'll second that," Susan said.

"Come on," I told Kari. She gave me a weird look but got up.

After we had walked away from the rest-house and the crush of people, she asked, "What was that all about?"

I paused. What was it I was going to say anyway? I hadn't really thought it out, and I hoped I hadn't made a mistake by dragging her off like this. She was looking at me expectantly, waiting for some kind of explanation.

"Well," I began, "when we were having our drinks, I saw this strange, far-away look on your face. Something about it reminded me of yesterday. Want to talk about it?"

"Boy, you don't miss a beat, do you?"

"Nope," I told her.

She kicked at a little stone. Even though her eyes were fastened on it, I sensed that she was looking inside herself instead of at the little rock.

"Have you ever wondered what happens when people die?" she asked.

"Sure. I think everyone has."

"I guess I'm a little like the Egyptians," Kari said, but I didn't know what she meant.

"How so?" I asked.

"Well, you know the way they piled all that stuff into the antechambers of the tombs for the afterlife? It was like they thought the dead people could really use those things." I nodded, and Kari continued with, "And their bodies. I mean, the way they preserved them and put them in elaborate tombs and tried to seal them away so they'd never be touched again."

"Yeah," I said. There were things I liked about the ancient Egyptian funeral practices and things I didn't. But I knew we were really talking about Kari, not Egyptians.

"Well, something about being in that chamber with King Tut's mummy did something to me," she said. She paused for a minute and then asked, "Beth, did you ever think about what happened to Granmary's body after she died?"

I had, and it had bothered me a lot at first.

"I did," I told her. "Has it been bothering you?"

"Yeah, a lot. That's what I meant when I said I was like the Egyptians. I think they got awfully hung-up on bodies and stuff. But something happened to me in that tomb. I mean, his body was there in that sar-cophagus, but it's like I realized that King Tut—his *essence*—went somewhere else ages ago. Maybe in the big picture, it doesn't matter that the body doesn't last."

"That's what I decided about Granmary," I said.

··············
189

"It's that special essence, the part that doesn't die, that's most important."

"Yeah, I think I can let that part go now." Then so quietly that I had to lean closer to hear her, she added, "I don't think I've done a very good job of honoring her."

"As long as the feelings are honest, Kari," I told her, "I don't know if there's a right or wrong way to honor a dead person. I mean, look at the ancient Egyptians again. Lots of modern people think it was stupid to leave all those belongings in a room next to the body, but I don't know how we can say that. They obviously believed in what they were doing. It was right for them. I think the best way you honor someone is by loving."

"Yeah," she said. "Death is really about life, isn't it?"

"That's how I see it," I told her. "Everything is like a continuum."

"So Granmary's essence lives on, partly in us."

I nodded. Then my eyes pooled as I remembered the special person we were talking about. I thought about the way she stood her ground to save the old-growth trees, the way she jumped right in to help people, and her zest for life that came out in the way she shared her wonderful travel tales, her talent with the crochet hook, and her people skills. I knew we were in Egypt because of her, not just because she thought we'd have fun, but because she wanted us to come together in some new, special way. It was Granmary through and through.

"You're crying," Kari noticed.

"Yeah. I was just remembering," I told Kari. The way she looked at me was comforting.

"You know," she said, "I'm going to concentrate upon honoring her in positive ways, through good memories and good actions."

"That's the way to go."

Kari kicked the stone again. When it skittered my way, I put my weight onto the walking stick and gingerly raised my foot.

Then I kicked it back to her.

Chapter Eighteen

The next morning after breakfast, Dad said, "I think you ladies each deserve a special keepsake from Luxor." Susan, Kari, and I looked at him with identical looks of anticipation. Who could turn down a present?

"That sounds intriguing, Bruce," Susan commented.

"Yeah, Bruce," Kari told him.

"What did you have in mind?" I asked.

"We don't have far to go to our destination. See that shop across the lobby?" he asked. There were actually several of them.

"Which one?" Susan asked.

"The jewelry shop, of course," he said playfully, as if it were a foregone conclusion.

"Those aren't regular souvenirs," I warned him. We had passed the shop over and over. It was the good stuff.

"Well, my girls don't have to settle for regular souvenirs. Besides, gold is a good buy in Egypt."

With that, we headed toward the high-class little shop. The Egyptian behind the counter nodded at us politely but didn't try to pressure us the way many of the others we'd run into had. He just let us browse.

"Isn't this a wonderful collection?" Susan remarked as she began looking into the glass cases.

"Everything is beautiful," I commented.

There were collars that reminded me of Cleopatra and Nefertiti, with real lapis lazuli, carnelian, and other semiprecious gems, scarabs in gold or inlaid with jewels, and a wide assortment of amulets.

I stopped to look at the amulets, or good-luck

charms. Wouldn't it be nice, I thought, if a person could wear an *ankh* to actually bring good luck and a long life, or a stylized, eye-shaped *udjat* to ward off snakebite, illness, and curses?

"Ooh, look at these!" Kari exclaimed from across the room. I walked over and immediately knew why she was so excited.

"Cartouches," I said as I looked into a display case filled with gleaming gold charms. Row upon row of dazzling rectangles with rounded corners lay on black velvet trays. Some were just blank lozenge-shaped pieces of precious metal waiting for personalization. Others were replicas of the real cartouches I had seen often, carved onto columns at Karnak or on the walls of the tombs. The replicas had distinctive hieroglyphs or symbols on them in raised gold to indicate a particular pharaoh's royal seal.

"Wow! They're neat," I agreed.

"Would you like to see them closer?" Dad asked. When we nodded, he motioned to the salesman, who came up to us. We looked at several before deciding. In the end, Kari chose a blank gold lozenge. The jeweler would fill in the blank with hieroglyphs to make her name.

My eyes were drawn to the finished replicas.

"That one!" I told the jeweler, pointing to a shining gold charm. Inside the shape was the profile of a very regal-looking pharaoh. He wore the double-crown and held an *ankh*, and the solar disc shone above him.

"May I see that one?" I asked. The salesman, who spoke English as perfectly as Asmie had, handed it to me. It was even prettier up close.

"Who is he?" I asked as I looked at the figure of the pharaoh.

The salesman took the piece of jewelry from me

and examined the cartouche.

"Seti I," he told me.

"Perfect," I said. I liked the idea because I remembered that Mrs. Brinion said she might work something about Seti I into her new book.

The salesman set aside Kari's and my choices.

"Thanks, Dad," I told him as I gave him a quick hug. Kari did the same thing.

"Now, what about you, Susan? What tickles your fancy?"

"Everything does," she laughed. She looked around for five minutes more before settling on a big golden *ankh* charm.

It didn't seem right that Dad didn't get anything, but he wasn't into jewelry, I knew. Maybe we could find something special for him before the trip was over.

When it came time to decide what to do that day, Dad and Susan already had it planned.

"Put on one of those outfits your mother bought you, Beth," Dad said. "I'm taking you for lunch at the Winter Palace."

"Kari and I have other plans," Susan told me. I got it then. Kari was going to talk to her mother about Granmary and her guilt feelings. I felt a certain weight lift from me. I knew Kari needed more talking— especially more insight—than I could ever give her, and Susan, of all people, knew how much Granmary had loved her great-granddaughter.

"Sounds good to me," I said.

Later, Dad and I took a horse-drawn carriage to the Winter Palace, which was a big, old-fashioned hotel right across the street from the Nile. I liked its long porch.

When I saw the wood inside, I remarked, "This reminds me of when we used to go to the hotel in Portland when I was little."

"It does," he agreed, and we were both lost for a few moments in the memories of a very little girl with her daddy.

Maybe it was that memory of old times that steered our conversation toward our relationship toward the end of our meal.

"Are you having a good time in Egypt?" Dad asked.

"Do you have to ask?" I asked with a laugh. "It's wonderful. The museums, the temples, the tombs. Wow, the list could go on and on. It was really neat of Granmary to do this."

"It certainly was. You know, she hoped it might bring you and Kari a little closer, among other things."

"Yeah, I figured that out," I told him.

"How are you two doing?" he asked.

"Better." A lot better, I thought, but I didn't want to say more and somehow jinx things.

"Well, that's good." He paused then and fidgeted a little before adding, "You know, I know this whole thing hasn't been easy for you. The divorce. My marrying Susan. Your getting a stepsister."

You can say that again, I thought.

"I'm proud of you for the way you've been handling it."

Something caught in my throat. I don't think I'd ever heard him say those words.

"Thanks, Dad," I told him. Boy, that was lame. I wanted to say so much more, but it just hadn't come out.

"You know," he went on, "I never dreamed your mother and I would end up getting divorced. I married for keeps. I'm sure she did, too."

"Then what happened?" I asked. I finally wanted to hear his version.

He thought for a few moments and shook his head.

"Beth, you probably won't believe this," he told me, "but I just don't know. We were happy enough for several years. Whatever it was was insidious. It snuck up on us. She got busy with her TV show, but it wasn't really that. Not the hours she spent on it, at any rate. No, it was . . . well . . . I guess we just stopped communicating."

"But you always seemed to talk about things," I reminded him. Stopped communicating? It didn't make sense.

"We did, but it was . . . oh, I don't know, almost like shop talk."

"Shop talk?"

"We talked about the yard, our taxes . . . you. But I stopped knowing how she really felt about issues and happenings. She got so closed off. And she stopped asking how my day had gone or how I felt. Then one birthday she gave me some peanut brittle. Peanut brittle? I hate the stuff. We'd been married all those years, and she didn't even know I hate nuts. Something just sort of died. Beth, we just didn't have anything to talk about anymore."

"You met Susan," I said.

"Yes, I met Susan, but all this other—I don't know what to call it—happened before I met her. There wouldn't have been a Susan in my life if your mother and I had had something growing and vital at home. With Susan, I could laugh again, and I could talk about things and have some response. Your mother may have loved me, but it's odd to say, I don't think she really *liked* me. Susan does."

Wow! What could I say? What happened to two people that things just sort of fizzled out?

Dad began talking again. "You like Susan, don't you?"

"Well, sure, Dad."

"Do I sense a 'but'? She wasn't like some kind of stereotypical woman out to get me."

I thought about Mom and her *that woman* talk. At first, I really had thought of Susan as wicked, but I knew that wasn't true now and that Mom had just been talking through her hurt and other emotions.

"I know that, Dad." Then I thought about being at their house and not knowing my role. Maybe it was time to dive in and say something about it. "Dad, I know Susan doesn't mean to make me feel like an outsider at your house, but sometimes I feel that way."

"Tell me about it," Dad said. He looked surprised that I felt that way.

"Well, it's just that I don't seem to fit in. I don't know what my role is when I'm there, like sometimes if I'm supposed to jump in and help out or just watch Kari and Susan. I feel like a guest."

Dad laughed, although not at me.

"Susan has been trying too hard. I know she never meant to make you feel so unsure of your position. When you are at our house, Beth, just remember that you are as much a daughter of the house as Kari is. The stepmother role is as new for her as your new roles are for you."

"I hadn't thought of it that way. Anyway, I do like her."

"Good."

"So, what's been happening in your life. Still going with Brad Brownlee?" he asked. He *was* way behind the times, and for a moment I felt my old irritation creep back. But then I realized he was asking, and that's more than he'd done for months.

I told him that Brad and I were no longer a couple.

"Is there someone else I should worry about?" he asked good-naturedly. He looked sort of uneasy as he added, "Your mother has filled you in on guys your age,

....
197

hasn't she?" Did he mean the birds and the bees?

"Yeah, she has, Dad." It felt funny to be talking about guys with my dad.

"So?" he asked, obviously waiting for something.

"So?"

"Is there someone else?" he asked again.

"Sort of," I told him, "but you don't have to worry about him. He has old-fashioned values."

"I'm glad to hear that."

Our lemon ices arrived, and we switched to small talk over dessert.

After lunch, when I'd come back from using the restroom, Dad said, "The man at the desk just told me that the museum doesn't open until four o'clock. It sounds as though it's worth waiting for. Shall we hang around?"

"Yeah," I said. I loved museums and knew this little one was supposed to be a gem. When I looked out the window and saw how pretty the Nile looked, I asked, "Why don't we cross the street and walk along the river until it's time to go?"

Dad thought it was a good idea. Fortunately, it wasn't quite as hot today, and it turned out to be a really pretty walk. The sun made the Nile sparkle, a breeze had the palm trees swaying, and we felt the mystique of the necropolis as it continually drew our gaze across the river.

"You do well with that walking stick," Dad observed.

"Yeah, I don't know what I'd have done without it at Karnak and the Valley of the Kings," I told him.

"It's a pretty thing."

"I know."

"It also opened my eyes to how you struggle just to walk. Beth, I'm sorry if I've been like an ostrich about your balance."

I wasn't going to say, Oh, that's ginger-peachy, Dad. His actions over the years had hurt me a lot and made me feel like a total klutz. But he was at least talking to me as he hadn't for a long, long time, and I didn't want to attack him.

"It always surprised me," I told him, "because you're so good about my hearing loss."

"Yeah, well, I've watched you all these years, Beth, and the hearing loss doesn't seem to be the handicap in your life that the balance thing is. I know it's no picnic not to hear right. I'm not trying to minimize that. But I watch your struggle with the balance thing."

He stopped and shook his head.

"Then why do you so often try to get me to do the things that I can't do?" I asked.

He hung his head, and I couldn't figure out what was going on in his mind. He finally looked up, but his eyes didn't meet mine.

"It's my fault," he told me.

"Your fault? About what?" I asked.

"That you can't hear right or walk right. I thought if I could just get you to play tennis or ride a camel or do any number of things that it would assuage my guilt."

"Dad, I really don't know why you'd feel guilty. I was sick, and those things just happened. It wasn't your fault."

"But it was," he said. His voice was anguished. I'd never heard that tone from him before, and I hurt for him. But I also had to know what he was talking about.

"Why?" I asked softly. "Please tell me."

"All right. Your mother knew you were sick. I did too. The difference is that her instinct told her you needed to go to the hospital. I talked her into calling Dr. Paulson. He, of course, asked your symptoms, and your mother told him. Most children with your kind of meningitis have a terribly high fever. At that point, you didn't, so the doctor wasn't alarmed. He told us just to make an appointment at his office and he'd see you. Mom wanted to take you to the hospital anyway, but I told her she was overreacting and that we should listen to the doctor. So, you see, it's my fault you got so sick. And I'm so, so sorry."

I tried to picture the scene. It had been a mother's instincts versus a father's trust in the doctor. No, I couldn't blame Dad.

"Dad?" I said. He was looking out over the Nile. I could see the outline of the necropolis, but somehow I knew he wasn't seeing that.

As he heard me call his name, he looked at me. I set my cane onto the bench and hugged him. Then I patted his back, like a mother does a little boy, and said, "It's okay." We pulled apart and I went on. "I'm the one who has to live with these things. If I don't blame you—and I don't—please don't blame yourself. If anyone is to blame, it was Dr. Paulson, but what good does blame do anyway? I am what I am. My life is good, Dad. I don't miss the tennis and stuff as much as I need to be accepted just the way I am."

"Don't expect me to change overnight, but I'll try to do that. I really will," he told me.

And I knew at that moment that it didn't matter how many times he played tennis with Kari, or how many things I couldn't do that he wanted me to. I had my father, and I finally understood where he'd been coming from all those years.

I was feeling very happy when we finally went to the Museum of Ancient Egyptian Art not far from the Winter Palace. As I looked at finds from the Thebes area, I was thinking more of Dad and me than of the colossal red granite head of Amenophis III, the gilded Hathor, or the stone statue of the crocodile god, Sobek.

Dad and Susan decided to make it their splurge night and have a romantic dinner out by themselves. Kari and I waved them off in one of the gharries, or horse-drawn carriages, and then went into the hotel's coffee shop to fill each other in on what had been happening.

Kari *had* talked to Susan about Granmary, and she was just as happy as I was for her that I'd had such a meaningful talk with Dad.

We were just finishing dinner when Mrs. Brinion walked into the coffee shop.

"Hello, Mrs. Brinion," I called out.

Kari waved.

"Hello, girls," she said as she walked purposefully toward our table. She had her ever-present totebag with her.

"How's the book coming?" I asked as she came up to us.

"Later," she cut off. She didn't seem like her usual, carefree self. "Beth, do you have your walking stick with you?"

"Sure. I practically always do," I told her. Why was she asking about my walking stick?

"Would you like to sit down with us?" Kari invited. Mrs. Brinion did.

"Thank you," she told Kari absently. Then to me she asked, "May I see the walking stick?"

I reached behind me and handed it to her.

"What's going on?" I asked her. Then I glanced at Kari, who just shrugged. My first guess was that it had caught her fancy and maybe she wanted to use one like it in her story, but she seemed too tense for that. Then again, what did I know anyway? Maybe writers did get that way when they were piecing things together.

"I'll have an answer for you in a moment," she told us.

With that, we watched as the writer looked up and down the stick's length, shook it gently, and finally started tapping the brass lotus top. "I won't hurt the stick," she assured me.

I nodded.

Then she began working with all her might to twist the lotus. It didn't budge, but she kept at it. I wanted to ask her a million questions. Instead, I just watched her busy hands and her face. Suddenly, her look of concentration changed.

"My word!" she exclaimed softly. She frowned, looked around the room furtively, and then we watched in amazement as she unscrewed the brass flower from the walking stick's shaft.

"How weird," Kari remarked.

"What is it?" I asked.

But Mrs. Brinion didn't comment. Instead, she took a linen hotel napkin and opened it. Then she spread it flat on top of the tablecloth.

"This is your answer," she said as something fell onto the napkin. It all happened so fast that I only had the impression of a cascade of red and blue and gold.

"Ooh, let me see," Kari said.

"No, not right now," Mrs. Brinion answered as she quickly wrapped what looked like pieces of jewelry into the napkin and popped the whole thing into her totebag. She screwed the lotus back onto the shaft of the walking stick.

"We can talk now. Beth, put the stick back where it was."

I did.

"Those were jewels!" I exclaimed.

Mrs. Brinion nodded.

"Tell me again how you came to get the stick," she demanded, and once again I related my fall and Asmie's thoughtful gift.

"Well, it was thoughtful, all right," Mrs. Brinion commented, "but not in the way you mean. Beth, I think you're being used as a dupe to move these jewels, which I suspect are not ordinary gemstones."

Something clicked in my mind. Blue and red and gold: lapis lazuli, carnelian, and real gold. How may times had I seen that very combination in the museums?

"They're something from ancient times!" I said in astonishment.

"Awesome!" Kari exclaimed, wide-eyed.

"They may well be," Mrs. Brinion told us. "You see, I've been doing research on my book— research that has included looking into smuggling artifacts out of Egypt. There are rings of smugglers that use innocent tourists to transport the stolen goods, you see. Your walking stick and how you got it as a gift flashed through my mind, and it just suddenly hit me that you could be being used as an unsuspecting courier."

"But why Beth?" Kari asked.

"Yeah, why me?"

"I can think of at least two reasons," the writer told us. "One, you're an almost perfect dupe because of your age. And two, you were in the right place at the right time. Beyond that, I have no idea, just as I have no idea what's really in that napkin. I could be way off the track, you know. It could be a stage prop and the 'jewels,' glass. But they may also be the real thing, and if they are, it's much too dangerous for you to keep carrying them. Let me take them to my room. Keep using the walking stick just as you have been."

"What will you do?" I asked.

"I have an acquaintance, an Inspector Khattab, who has helped me immeasurably with my research. I want to give him a call and let him take it from there. May I take the contents of your stick?"

"Yeah, I guess that's a good plan," I told her.

....

"But you'll call our room as soon as you hear anything, won't you?" Kari asked.

For the first time that evening, Mrs. Brinion gave us a smile.

"Of course, I will. I'm sure he will want to talk to you, too," she said. She looked at our dinner plates and added, "Good, I see you are finished, or about so, with your dinners. I think you should go back to the safety of your room, or to your parents' room, until you hear from me."

And with that, she grabbed her bag and was leaving. I quickly signed the dinner tab, and then we were up and on our way to our room. By the time we reached the bank of elevators, Mrs. Brinion was nowhere in sight.

"It's like something out of a movie," Kari commented as we waited for the elevator.

"Or one of her books," I amended as the door opened.

Then we were on our way up. I looked at the now-empty walking stick. Who would have thought it had held anything? Of course, as Mrs. Brinion had reminded us, it could be a stage prop. Yeah, that had to be it. People no doubt found artifacts to smuggle, but what were the chances of *my* getting involved? Yeah, it had to be something like a magician's prop. I relaxed. No doubt Mrs. Brinion's research had given her an over-active imagination. Still, it would be interesting to see how it played out.

The elevator door eased open. I always looked both ways before stepping out, in order not to get bowled over by someone not looking where he was going. You'd be surprised at the way people don't even look. Nothing to my left. Than I looked to my right just as the elevator whispered shut behind us. Something like an electric current charged through me.

Brown Suit! It was unmistakably the same man, and to my horror, I saw that he was following Mrs. Brinion down the hallway. I had to do something. But what?

"Kari," I whispered. I put my finger to my lips. "Don't say a word. Brown Suit! He's following Mrs. Brinion. Get someone to help. I'm going after him."

"But—" she started to protest.

"Just go. There's no time to argue," I insisted. She nodded. I saw her press the DOWN button as I started down the hallway.

Would Brown Suit look back? Then an even more horrible thought crossed my mind: *Did he have a gun?* I froze, but only momentarily. Even if he did, I couldn't let him hurt Mrs. Brinion. Two of us against him had a better chance than one seventy-ish lady.

Mrs. Brinion was unlocking her room door as Brown Suit neared her. Should I call out and warn her? Or would that just do more harm than good? Kari should be back soon, I decided. The best thing to do might be to stall for time.

I plastered myself against a hallway wall and watched as her key turned in the lock. Just as her door was opening, Brown Suit hurried up to her and she became aware of him. They began to tussle.

Don't fail me now, Kari, I thought.

I couldn't wait for the police. I hurried to Mrs. Brinion's room and got there just in time to see Brown Suit push the writer into her room. She looked dazed but otherwise unhurt, and by the way Brown Suit left the door wide open, I guessed he was only after the jewels, not Mrs. Brinion.

I thought fast, looking to my right and left. Only two doors past Mrs. Brinion's room the hallway intersected with another hallway. I suddenly had an idea.

As I carefully passed the room, Brown Suit was rummaging through the totebag. It gave me just enough time to slip past the open door and make it to the intersecting hallways.

I got down low and grabbed my walking stick for dear life. Would Brown Suit even come this way? I knew the stairs were over here. Or would he take the elevator back down? Well, if he took the elevator, Kari and help would probably be there to stop him. But if I were Brown Suit, I thought, I'd use the stairs. More chances to get away. I wouldn't want to get caught in a little moving cubicle.

I listened hard for footsteps, but the carpet muffled most sounds. Fortunately, I was sensitive to vibrations, and as it happened, it was vibration rather than sound that clued me in. Suddenly, I tasted something like metal in my mouth. Fear, I knew.

Brown Suit was coming!

I peeked around the corner just enough to verify who it was. I saw just enough to know that baggy, brown-trousered legs were coming my way fast. My heart felt like it was going two hundred beats a minute. Don't faint, I told myself.

Now! I commanded myself. Just as he got to the intersection, I stuck out the walking stick and held onto it hard.

I felt it almost wrench from my hands as he hit it. Brown Suit let out a grunt and an Arabic word. Then, as if in slow motion, the length of his body fell and the napkin filled with jewels flew out of his grasp.

Could I grab it in time and get away with it?

Kari, where are you? Please come, I begged silently.

I lunged for the jewel-filled napkin and got it, but I couldn't move fast enough. Brown Suit was suddenly on me, reaching for the little white ball of antiquity. He was squeezing my arm so hard that I thought it would break.

"You leave me alone!" I shouted over my pain. I had to hang on, had to hang on . . . .

Just as I knew I'd have to give in, I heard a voice yell:

"Don't you hurt my sister!" *Kari!*

Then she and I were pummeling Brown Suit for all we were worth. It seemed like we were keeping him down, but it didn't last. He was just starting to get up when Mrs. Brinion also came running down the hall. Were those the police way back down the hall?

"You evil man!" she told him. Then she started hitting him with her book-heavy totebag. I grabbed my walking stick and caned him. Kari used her fists.

Whether or not we would have kept him down is anybody's guess because fortunately help reached us from two sides. A security guard came from the direction of the elevator, just as another man came running from the door to the stairs. I'm sure that Kari and Mrs. Brinion sighed just as heavily as I did. It was over at last.

Brown Suit was theirs.

Chapter Nineteen

When he gave me this travel journal, Matt wished me an unforgettable trip, and it certainly was one—in more ways than one!

First of all, I got to see Karnak, the Pyramids of Giza—all the places of my dreams— and they were even better than I'd imagined they'd be. History will never seem the same to me, and I shall always treasure my own personal discovery of such a wondrous land and its art, architecture, and spirit.

Secondly, I finally feel that Dad and I have connected on a new, important level. I have a better idea where he's been coming from all these years.

Then there was the unexpected intrigue. Boy, would Granmary have loved the story of Asmie, Brown Suit, and the walking stick filled with jewels! I'll never forget Dad and Susan's faces when they returned to the hotel that night and casually asked if anything exciting had happened while they were gone.

Along with Mrs. Brinion, of course, Kari and I had talked to the police about our strange adventure. Brown Suit had been arrested, but Asmie, as it turned out, had quit work at the hotel in Giza. He'd never surfaced and might have fled the country, it was thought.

The most incredible thing was that the items

inside the walking stick really had been jewels.

Whether or not they were ancient ones hadn't been determined for sure, but Inspector Khattab, Mrs. Brinion's friend, had said they could very well be from the fabulous Murdoch Collar, an ancient artifact that had disappeared during World War II. Tests would tell the tale.

"Whatever they turn out to be," our writer friend had told us, "this is more exciting than anything I was putting into my book."

I didn't think the police would let me take the walking stick home with me. I wasn't even sure I wanted it after what had happened. But they let me have it, and now I'm glad I'd taken it. Not only is it unusual to look at, with its notorious history, but it's helped me so much when I walk that I've gotten quite used to using it. Call it a cane or a walking stick: I wouldn't be too proud and put away something that improved my mobility.

And last but not least, as Granmary certainly knew when she sent us to Egypt, being cooped up with Kari in such a different environment had been a catalyst to a new, much better relationship.

"Don't you hurt my sister!" she had warned Brown Suit.

As the plane soared above the snow-frosted peaks, I put down my pen and looked over at Kari. Relationships aren't made overnight. I knew our troubles probably weren't entirely over. Still, when she looked at me and sort of smiled, I guessed that, for better or worse, I'd found a sister.

I smiled back.

THE END